His arms tightened around her and she laid her head back on his shoulder as the torch singer exaggerated every sultry note.

Josette quit talking or thinking and melted into the desire that encompassed her. The song ended long before she was ready.

Another ballad started and she stayed in his arms. This time they barely moved, but just swayed together, holding on to each other, so close the hunger inside her grew dangerously unbridled.

The band took their break after that song. She and Keenan were the last to leave the floor.

It was just a dance, she reminded herself. They were strangers in the night, caught up in a magical infatuation that was too new to trust though too hot to ignore.

They were only in New Orleans for three more days.

FRENCH QUARTER FATALE

JOANNA WAYNE

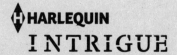

To my friends and family who love a good crawfish boil, Cajun festival and po'boy stuffed with fried oysters any day.

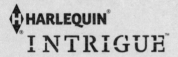

INTRIGUE™

ISBN-13: 978-1-335-58250-8

French Quarter Fatale

Copyright © 2023 by Jo Ann Vest

Recycling programs for this product may not exist in your area.

For questions and comments about the quality of this book, please contact us at CustomerService@Harlequin.com.

Harlequin Enterprises ULC
22 Adelaide St. West, 41st Floor
Toronto, Ontario M5H 4E3, Canada
www.Harlequin.com

Printed in U.S.A.

Joanna Wayne began her professional writing career in 1994. Now, more than fifty published books later, Joanna has gained a worldwide following with her cutting-edge romantic suspense and Texas family series, such as Sons of Troy Ledger and Big "D" Dads. Joanna currently resides in a small community north of Houston, Texas, with her husband. You may connect with her at joannawayne.com.

Books by Joanna Wayne

Harlequin Intrigue

New Orleans Noir
French Quarter Fatale

The Kavanaughs

Riding Shotgun
Quick-Draw Cowboy
Fearless Gunfighter
Dropping the Hammer

Big "D" Dads: The Daltons

Trumped Up Charges
Unrepentant Cowboy
Hard Ride to Dry Gulch
Midnight Rider
Showdown at Shadow Junction
Ambush at Dry Gulch

Visit the Author Profile page at Harlequin.com.

CAST OF CHARACTERS

Josette Guillory—Her mother is missing and she is falling in love with an FBI agent.

Keenan Carter—An FBI counterterrorist agent who's out to protect Josette with his life.

Antoine Guillory—A shrimper, Josette's father and possible suspect in her mother's disappearance.

Homicide Detective Max Hyde—He backs down to no one.

Lorraine Cormier—Owns the shrimp and crab shack and the bayou fishing cabins.

Prologue

It was Mardi Gras season in New Orleans, a time when masked revelers riding on giant floats ruled the streets. A time when children sat atop Mardi Gras ladders lined up in long rows to better catch the action while everyone around them fought over doubloons and the cheap plastic beads flying from the hands of the parade riders.

And in the "anything goes" Vieux Carré, female tourists and locals alike traded modesty for the daring lifting of their shirts to offer quick glimpses of body parts usually kept hidden while in public.

But that wasn't the scene in front of the watcher. No parades and revelry here. Just the stifling humidity and threatening wildlife of the bayou.

The watcher walked a few feet farther and the ground slowly leveled into a deepening quagmire.

An owl gave its forlorn call, the screech echoing around it.

A long black snake slithered through the bog, passing mere inches away.

The watcher didn't give it a second look. Growing

up on the bayou, you learn early which vipers are dangerous.

Learning which people were treacherous was not that easy. Figuring out whom you could trust was damn near impossible.

And getting mixed up with the wrong person could be deadly.

Chapter One

Josette Guillory rummaged in her handbag until she pulled out her vibrating phone. Her best friend's name popped up on the screen.

Addison Landry, likely making sure Josette hadn't backed out of her commitment.

"Hello, Addison. Have no fears," Josette greeted. "I'll be on the plane when it arrives in New Orleans."

"I never doubted you. Have you boarded yet?"

"No, but the plane's here and we have a crew. Looks like we'll be on time."

"Perfect. You might want to grab a nap on the flight. Party starts the minute you arrive in the Big Easy."

"I'm sure the party is already in full swing."

Even if it weren't Mardi Gras weekend, the fun seldom slowed down with Addison around. Josette hadn't met the intended groom yet but hoped Bart Gordon had enough spark and energy to keep up with his soon-to-be wife without curtailing her adventuresome spirit.

Either way, Josette couldn't wait to meet him. All she knew for certain was that Addison was madly in love. Not for the first time, or even the dozenth time, but the first time she'd gotten anywhere near the "I do" stage.

"I'll take a taxi to the hotel," Josette volunteered, "but it may take a while. Traffic must be a nightmare with the first of the Friday night parades getting set to roll."

"Worse than a nightmare. I wouldn't do that to you. Bart will pick you up at baggage claim. Just look for the sexy hunk wearing a Saints hat."

"Ah. Sexy hunks are always easy to spot. Let him know I'm in a purple dress with tall black boots."

"I've already told him that you'll be the most stylishly dressed, gorgeous woman around."

"You can save the flattery. I'm already fully committed to the whole maid-of-honor shebang."

"And you can't imagine how much I appreciate that. I know the location and the timing are bummers for you," Addison admitted, her voice suddenly taking on a more sober tone.

Right on both counts, Josette thought. As a uniformed agent took her place behind the gate podium, Josette couldn't prevent her mind from traveling to her mother. The last time Josette or anyone else had seen or even heard from Isadora Guillory was almost exactly a year ago. Isadora had been celebrating Mardi Gras in the French Quarter when she simply disappeared.

Few of her fans and admirers had been totally shocked, least of all Josette. Disappearing when things weren't going exactly her way had always been Isadora's modus operandi.

The practice went all the way back to when Josette was three years old and Isadora deserted her and her hardworking father to go "find herself" in New York.

Isadora had not only found herself, but in the process she became one of the wealthiest and most successful TV actresses around.

But for the eccentric Isadora, it seemed that the more famous she became, the more she felt the need to escape her current life for a new adventure, usually with a new lover. Weeks in the remote South Pacific with a swarthy tycoon. Months in Iceland with a former foreign minister.

Isadora would eventually just show up one morning and make certain her publicists were immediately aware of her return. Her ardent fans would go berserk, and the writers of her TV show would find some miracle way to convince the viewers that she'd never really died. She'd get written back into the script with a huge advance in pay.

Not this time, Josette thought as a wave of goose bumps ascended her spine. Her mother had been gone an entire year, almost to the very day. She'd never disappeared that long.

For the past few months, Josette had tried telling herself Isadora had finally found her happy place— wherever that was. But she couldn't prevent the chilling doubt that swept her. Had her mother met with foul play?

Not only did Josette worry about her mother but

she was sick and tired of getting threatening calls and letters accusing her of killing Isadora so she could inherit her mother's millions.

As passengers started lining up to board, Josette determinedly pushed Isadora from her mind. At least she tried to. She didn't want anything to spoil her weekend with Addison on her special day.

It would be a short flight from Nashville to New Orleans, no real need to fly first class. But the Landrys were treating this as a destination wedding, even though they lived in a mansion on St. Charles Avenue, just a short ride from the French Quarter. They were footing the bill for all the expenses for the wedding party, including lodging in a luxury hotel in the heart of the old square or Vieux Carré.

Only the best for their only daughter.

Once on the plane, Josette found her window seat quickly: 4A. She lifted her small, flowered duffel bag to fit it into the overhead bin. But as the strap caught on the armrest, she teetered and the luggage bounced into the aisle seat, which was thankfully still empty.

She turned, looked up and found herself staring into a pair of ginger-brown eyes that seemed to tease without trying.

"Do you need some help with that?" the man asked, his voice deep and masculine.

"Thanks, but I can get it," she murmured as she untangled the strap and fitted the luggage into the compartment.

"Ah, an independent woman."

His half grin was wickedly sexy.

"Sorry," she taunted. "I can take it out of the bin and let you put it in again if that will make you feel more manly."

He seemed to stifle a laugh. "That's a thought, but you could just let me buy you a drink."

"They're free in this section."

"In that case, I'll buy you two."

Her grin matched his. "What a gentleman," she said archly. "But I'll be sticking to a cola. Don't want to get tipsy before I reach Bourbon Street."

Her arm brushed his shoulder as she slid into her seat. A ridiculous rush of awareness zinged along her nerve endings. She resolutely ignored it. This weekend was about catching up with her bestie and celebrating her happiness. Not reveling in the attention of a good-looking man.

He lingered in the aisle. "Will this be your first Mardi Gras?"

"No," she said, "but the first in several years, so the first since I can legally flash an ID at the bar."

"Good. I understand flashing is an integral part of celebrating the festival to its fullest."

She'd say this. The man knew how to flirt. The glint in his eye made it hard to resist. But she tried. "So I've heard, but the ID is all I'll be flashing. I'm not into cheap beads."

"Smart woman. Hold out for the fancy throws or the Moon Pies. By the way, my name's Keenan, in case you need help with your misbehaving luggage again."

"I'll try to keep it under control."

She didn't volunteer her name. She was always

wary of strangers, even ones as sexy as Keenan. She never knew if they were interested in her for herself or her mother's money and fame.

A middle-aged man in a dark gray business suit stopped in the aisle next to where Keenan was blocking his access to the overhead bin. The man pointed to the empty seat next to Josette. "Excuse me but I believe that's my seat."

"No problem," Keenan said. "We were just chatting. My seat's a couple of rows up." He stepped out of the way.

Her legitimate seatmate paused. "If you'd like, I'll be happy to change seats with you," he offered. "I'm traveling alone."

"That's nice of you." Keenan stared at Josette, his brows arched, waiting for her to respond.

"We're not together," she answered quickly. "But thanks for offering."

Keenan stepped out of the man's way but kept his eyes locked with Josette's. "Perhaps we'll run into each other on Bourbon Street this weekend," he said.

"In the midst of thousands of revelers?"

He smiled. "You never know."

As he walked toward his seat, she noticed a limp in his left leg. Whatever the physical problem, it hadn't detracted from his charisma or the way he fit into his jeans and solid black knit pullover.

Perhaps she'd been a bit hasty in turning down the opportunity to chat with him during the flight. What harm could there possibly have been if she'd remained anonymous—which, unfortunately, she almost never did.

She was above all Isadora Guillory's daughter and except for their hair color and age difference, they looked incredibly alike. Well, that did exaggerate the fact a bit.

No one was as knockout a beauty as Isadora.

THE LADY WAS a looker, a real Cajun beauty unless Keenan missed his guess. Hair as dark as midnight, falling past her shoulders and down her back.

Seductive, dark lashes, flawless complexion, a tempting mouth made for kissing. Damn near perfection.

He hadn't intended to hit on her, but she was too stunning for any unattached, red-blooded, straight guy like himself to ignore.

Not to mention, she wasn't wearing a gold band to declare her off-limits.

He fastened his seat belt. The flight attendant reached past him to hand his seatmate a drink before taking Keenan's order for a Scotch on the rocks.

"Do you know who that lady was you were just talking to?" the man sitting beside him asked when the attendant walked away.

"Should I?"

"Ever heard of Isadora Guillory?"

"Sounds familiar." He gave it some thought. "Is she the TV star who went missing from New Orleans last year?"

"That's the one. Do you see the resemblance now?"

"Yes, but as I remember it, the missing actress was a good deal older than the beauty on our flight."

"Yep," the man agreed. "But she's just the right age to be her daughter. I'd put money on it that she is."

The attendant returned with Keenan's drink. He thanked her and took a long sip. He searched his memory before turning back toward the guy with all the info.

He remembered the Bureau had been involved in the investigation of the actress, who had gone missing a year ago. But the last he'd heard through the grapevine, the police and the FBI had found no evidence of foul play. Of course, that might have changed by now. After all, the world was a small place, especially for someone as famous and recognizable as Isadora Guillory. She couldn't have just fallen off the face of the earth.

His seatmate swallowed a mouthful of his pale ale, then continued. "You know, Isadora's daughter is set to inherit a fortune if her mother turns up dead."

"You seem to know a great deal about the Guillorys. Are you a friend of theirs?" Keenan asked.

"Nope, never lucky enough to meet either one of them, but my wife never missed that TV show. I watched it with her sometimes just to look at Isadora. Know what I mean?" he asked with a waggle of his eyebrows.

Keenan knew what he meant, and if Isadora was half the beauty the woman in 4A was, he could understand why.

Any other time, Keenan would have been tempted

to check out the Isadora Guillory mystery on his laptop. But not today. He had no time or desire to go looking for crime in all the wrong places.

Not only was this practically his last week of rehab leave, but also it was party time, the perfect opportunity to hang out with the best group of old college buddies a guy could have.

He planned to make the most of it.

Who are you kidding? That devilish voice inside his head spoke up. *You can never ignore a mystery.*

Chapter Two

Approximately two hours later, Keenan's plane taxied to the gate at Louis Armstrong Airport. Passengers began to bustle, releasing seat belts, turning on phones and gathering their belongings from seat pockets.

As soon as the buzzer sounded, they squeezed into the aisle to collect their carry-on bags. He was right in there with them, ready to deboard the 707 and stretch his stiff leg.

Keenan spotted Bart from the escalator on his way down to baggage claim. They'd been as close as brothers in Louisiana State University, but that had been several years ago.

The last time he'd seen Bart had been when they'd gotten together with two of their LSU teammates for a fly-fishing trip in Colorado last year.

Great times where they'd done as much drinking and reliving the old glory days on the gridiron as they had casting in the cold mountain stream. Both Moose and Lance were with them then and they'd be here this weekend, as well.

Bart saw Keenan, grinned and rushed over. The

greeting quickly progressed into a vigorous half hugging, half back clapping.

"The quarterback has arrived. Let the games begin," Bart said.

"Where's Moose and Lance?" Keenan asked as they walked toward the luggage carousel.

"You're it, so far. Moose is flying in tomorrow."

"Bringing a girlfriend?"

"No. I think he just broke up with one."

"What about Lance?"

"Driving down from Shreveport tomorrow afternoon."

"With his wife?"

"No, Candace can't make it. Her sister is expecting her first child any day now, and his wife wants to make sure she's there for it. He's driving home first thing Tuesday morning."

"Missing Fat Tuesday? That's not like the Lance of old. Marriage must be taming him."

"Apparently, but he sounds happy."

Keenan switched his backpack to his other shoulder. "What about you? Feet cold yet?"

"Nope. Not even cool. My super-hot fiancée sees to that."

Keenan punched his friend's arm in a playful gesture. "Always said you were the luckiest guy in the game. You're still proving me right."

"So, when are you going to take the plunge into marital bliss?" Bart asked.

"When I find a woman like the fiancée you keep

bragging about. I can't wait to meet Addison. Is she here with you?"

"No. She's waiting for us at the hotel in the Quarter, finalizing plans for the next few days. She and the wedding planner have been practically joined at the hip for the last couple of months. I stay as far from all of that as I can."

The carousel buzzer sounded. Keenan's luggage was the first one down the chute. He grabbed it and backed out of the way. Normally, carry-on luggage would have been all he needed. This time, though, the formal events required more.

He started to walk away but Bart remained in place. His eyes scanned the area.

"Looking for someone else?" Keenan asked.

"Yeah. I'm also picking up Addison's maid of honor. You two were supposed to be on the same flight."

"She wouldn't happen to have long black hair and dynamite curves, would she?" Keenan asked.

"I haven't met her yet," Bart admitted, "but that sounds about the way Addison described her."

"Wearing a vibrant purple dress and high boots with nosebleed heels?" Kennan added.

Bart nodded. "So, you did meet her."

"Not exactly. We wrestled over her carry-on. She won."

"There's got to be a story there."

"Yep. How much of one remains to be seen."

As if on cue, the mystery lady appeared at Bart's elbow. "Are you by any chance Bart Gordon?"

"Yes, and you must be Josette Guillory."

That tightened the knot of possibility that she was the daughter of the missing Isadora Guillory but didn't guarantee it. After all, Guillory was a common name in Louisiana.

Besides, it was kind of strange that Bart hadn't mentioned the relationship if it was real.

"This is Keenan Carter," Bart offered. "My best man and—"

"Wait a sec. That's my bag," Josette interrupted the introduction as she pointed at an oversize, bright blue hardcase spinner passing them by on the carousel. She tried to squeeze past the others waiting for their luggage but wasn't quick enough.

Keenan made the luggage rescue. It weighed a ton. She must have packed her whole closet. He wondered if there were any other sexy boots in there.

THE GUYS TALKED nonstop on the walk to the short-term parking lot, giving Josette a chance to settle down. When she'd left Nashville, she thought she was okay with being in New Orleans. But the thought of stepping into the same city where her mother was last seen, on the same weekend, was proving too much of a distraction. She couldn't stop thinking of it. Missing her mother and, more so, fearing what had happened to her. The past few days she hadn't been able to shake the theory that Isadore had been taken against her will.

But why?

Josette didn't have a chance to ponder the reason. Bart stopped them beside a black luxury SUV and used his remote to open the rear hatch. "Our chariot for the day, provided by Addison's dad so that I can offer private taxi service for arriving wedding guests."

"Way to live," Keenan said as he assessed the SUV. He loaded their bags, then opened the passenger-side door for Josette before settling in the back seat himself. Bart pulled into a line of traffic.

"How did you and Addison meet?" Keenan questioned Josette.

She twisted enough so that she could face him, noticing his left leg hitched awkwardly on the seat.

"Addison had the misfortune to get stuck with me as a roommate our first year at LSU. I was from New York and desperately homesick. Addison was an hour and a half from home and knew all the right people. She took me under her wing."

"If you lived in New York, how did you end up at LSU?"

"My parents are separated and have been most of my life, just never got divorced. My dad's a shrimper who lives on Bayou Lafourche. I thought going to school in Baton Rouge was a good opportunity for me to bond with him."

"Did you?"

She was surprised by his prying question. And even more surprised that she answered it. For the past year she'd avoided meeting new people and venturing out of her Nashville design studio, for fear of the prying questions and guilty speculations. People were eager to either probe her theories of her mother's disappearance or outright accuse her of foul play. And that included law enforcement. She avoided them most of all.

"To some extent we did bond," she told him. "He's a fascinating man, but seldom ventures far from his life as a shrimper."

Even more surprising, it appeared Keenan didn't know that she was Isadora Guillory's daughter. That wouldn't last long, but Josette would enjoy noncelebrity status as long as she could.

"When did you graduate from LSU?" Keenan asked.

"Last May."

"Unfortunately, by the time she and Addison were freshmen, we'd already graduated," Bart told Keenan as he shot him a look in the rearview. "They missed our infamous athletic exploits."

"And here I thought we were legends to be remembered forever," Keenan joked. "I'm sure you've enlightened Addison by now as to how great we were."

"I've tried. For some strange reason, she doesn't want to hear every elaborate detail about every touchdown pass I caught from you. But then she's not too keen about discussing my law cases, either."

"What about you, Keenan?" Josette asked. "Are you a football player turned attorney, too?"

"Not a chance. Attorneys spend way too much time cooped up in stuffy offices. Even though I was only at the university for football, I did manage to get a degree in criminal justice while I was there."

Bart slowed to let an eighteen-wheeler pull into

the traffic. "But on the bright side, no one shoots at me—except verbally."

"Good point," Keenan agreed. "What's the plan for this evening?" he asked before Josette could ask about the being-shot-at comment.

"A reasonably slow night," Bart said. "Cocktails at the hotel with Addison's parents and a few of their friends, followed by dinner for the four of us at Mr. B's Bistro. After that, it's just whatever trouble we can get into in the French Quarter."

"I can handle that," Keenan said, "as long as there's not too much walking. Leg tends to give out before I do."

"Then we'll take it easy tonight. The rest of the wedding party arrives tomorrow. After that the schedule of activities barely allows time to go to the bathroom. Sorry to be so crude, Josette, but that's only a slight exaggeration."

"As long as I get my coffee in the mornings, I'm up for anything," she said. "Now can we back up to the point where Keenan gets shot at with real bullets?"

"That was extremely overstated," Keenan said. "I actually have a strong dislike for any type of firearms, especially ones pointed at me."

"Keenan's an FBI agent," Bart said. "One of the best in the business. You probably read about his preventing a major terrorist attack in the DC area a few months ago."

"I *helped* in the case," Keenan corrected him. "That was a team effort. The other agents were smart enough not to get in the path of exploding shrapnel."

He patted the leg that was slightly hitched on the seat between them.

Bart started explaining but Josette didn't hear any of the details. Her ears had stopped working once they processed the salient fact. Keenan Carter was a hotshot FBI agent. Her anonymity was doomed.

Was he another of the law enforcement officers trying to get "insider info" on Isadora? Or worse yet, attempting to find evidence that she was guilty or complicit in her mother's disappearance and potential murder? She'd had more than her fill of them and felt herself sliding even closer to the car door at her left.

Too bad. Keenan Carter could have been a handsome distraction.

"No more talk about business," Keenan said, cutting off his friend. "From this second on, all talk of the FBI, bullets or crimes of any kind is off-limits. I'm strictly here to stand beside you when of your own volition you sign up for a lifetime ball and chain."

Relieved to hear that, Josette let out the breath she wasn't aware she was holding. Assuming, of course, Keenan was telling the truth.

"No ball and chain, but I may want to borrow your handcuffs some night," Bart joked.

"Anytime." Keenan turned back to face Josette. "What do you do in Nashville?"

"I'm a struggling fashion designer."

"She sells herself short," Bart corrected. "Addison tells me she's an awesome designer on her way to the top. Wait till you see the gowns she created for herself and the two bridesmaids. They'll only be outshone by my beautiful bride herself, of course."

Keenan looked her way and nodded his head to the side. "I look forward to being awed."

As Bart changed the subject back to old football tales, Josette leaned back and watched the passing scenery. Thoughts of her mother invaded her mind as they headed toward the French Quarter.

Isadora had invited Josette to join her in the Big Easy for the Mardi Gras festivities that night. Josette lived in regret that she hadn't accepted. It was seldom that Isadora invited Josette to do anything with her. If she'd accepted that invitation, would Isadora have disappeared that night?

Quicker than expected, Keenan, Bart and Josette entered the lavishly decorated hotel lobby. The carnival spirit rang with laughter, excited voices and music from a grand piano at the far end of the crowded lobby.

Huge bouquets of flowers accented in shades of gold, green and purple adorned every surface. Wildly festooned feathered masks decorated the walls.

Addison had warned her a few days ago that they would be in the same hotel her mother had stayed in last year. Not by intention, but it was the hotel Addison's father always used when he had clients in town. And it was super convenient for the wedding events.

Her heart pounded as she scanned the lobby, imagining her mother holding court among adoring fans, unaware that someone lurked on the outskirts, intent on doing her harm. Before the scenario could fully play out, Josette spotted Addison a few yards away. Her best friend hurried to her, squealing like a teenager when she pulled Josette into a hug.

"I'm so glad you're finally here," Addison said. "We have so much to talk about. Can you even believe I'm getting married?"

She shed the morbid visions and pasted on a smile. "I can now that I've met Bart."

"Didn't I tell you he's wonderful?"

"Not over a few million times."

"We're both thrilled you're here," Bart echoed. "My ability to discuss veils, bouquets and music selections has been reduced to meaningless jargon. I hereby turn those responsibilities totally over to the maid of honor."

He introduced Keenan to Addison and after the four of them exchanged a bit of small talk, Bart took charge. "I'll take care of the luggage and get Keenan checked in," he said.

"I should check in, too," Josette said.

"Already taken care of," Addison said. "You and I are styling big-time. We're sharing the two-bedroom Princess Suite. Indulgence to the hilt and a fabulous corner balcony. We'll join up with you two guys in the hotel lounge when we meet my parents and their friends for cocktails at six."

"Works for me," Keenan said.

Bart gave Addison a quick kiss and the guys headed toward the check-in counter, Bart's luggage in tow.

Josette kept pace with Addison as they walked toward a wide, curving staircase. Despite her resolve, she couldn't resist one last view of the lobby. She noticed a familiar-looking young man across the lobby. By the time she put a name with the face, he was already walking away.

Just as well. Harley Broussard was from Alligator Cove, the fishing village where her dad lived. She'd made it a point not to tell Antoine she'd be in New Orleans this weekend, and she didn't want Harley to blow that.

These few days belonged to Addison, and it was awkward being with her dad. She loved her parents, but she'd never understood their on-again, off-again relationship. Probably never would. Besides, it was nearly impossible for her to stay positive around her dad since Isadora had vanished. Not when every day that passed made it clearer that she wasn't coming home.

Chapter Three

Once Keenan was checked in and the luggage had been herded to the right rooms, he and Bart found a table in the lobby lounge.

The cocktail waitress brought the lagers they'd ordered and poured them into icy mugs before leaving them alone again.

Bart took a swig and leaned back in his chair. "So, what do you think of my gorgeous bride-to-be?" Bart asked.

"I think she's gorgeous."

"Also, intelligent, witty and fun to be with," Bart added.

"That pretty much sums up perfection," Keenan said.

"Yeah. The amazing thing is, she loves me." He shrugged. "Go figure."

"Now that part is a mystery," Keenan joked, "but I predict you two will have a house full of rugrats soon, get rich and still be rocking on the porch together when you're ninety."

"Let's don't rush the kids and rocking chairs. I'm thinking a nice cutter for sailing on Lake Pontchartrain and several rounds of golf in Ireland and Scotland before we start changing diapers."

"Sounds like you have it all worked out."

"Not completely, but I don't have a doubt that Addison is the one for me. The thought of waking up with her every morning for the rest of my life is downright exciting."

Keenan got the whole happy-ever-after marriage mindset. His parents had it. So did his grandparents, who still held hands in their seventies. He just didn't see it happening to him, at least not anytime soon.

His life was the FBI and right now that meant protecting the country from terrorists, both homegrown and foreign. He never knew what town he'd be waking up in, much less whose bed. Everything he did was top secret. That was not conducive to a happy marriage.

He'd learned that from the several coworkers who'd tried to make a go of marriage. However, that didn't mean he couldn't appreciate a mysterious, stunningly seductive woman when one dropped into his life. Keenan took another satisfying gulp of his cold beer. "Tell me more about Josette Guillory."

"She's single."

"That's good for starters. Is she kin to Isadora Guillory, the missing TV star?"

"You are good," Bart said, raising his glass in a mock salute. "Did you recognize her or did the name give it away?"

"Was it supposed to be a secret?"

"No. Addison favored the idea of keeping the whole

missing mother/FBI scenario secret, for Josette's sake, but I convinced her it wouldn't work. Too many people know the details."

"You got that right. A gossipy seatmate on the plane saw me helping Josette with her luggage and filled me in. Says Josette stands to inherit millions when Isadora dies."

Bart whistled low. "That's a lot of money. Where does she stand with the FBI investigation?"

"As far as I know, the case went cold months ago. Whether that's true or not, I'm only here to make sure you and Addison make it to the altar."

"Now you're talking. I noticed you're still limping, though. How's your leg?"

"It hurts occasionally. Worse part is it slows me down. Best part is I'll live unless I crash into another booby-trapped situation." Several months ago, thanks to his undercover work, Keenan and his team had pinpointed the location of a terrorist who'd been planning an attack on Congress. But when they entered the abandoned warehouse where the extremist had holed up, none of them had been aware of the trip wire that triggered an explosion. Luck was with them that day and they hadn't lost a single agent, though Keenan was among the wounded. The leg injury had taken longer to heal than he'd hoped, but he looked at it this way: he was alive.

"It amazes me that you can joke about it, buddy," Bart said.

"I couldn't for the first few weeks."

The waitress stopped by to see if they wanted another drink. They refused. They still had cocktails scheduled with Addison's parents and dinner at one of the most popular restaurants in the Vieux Carré.

Along with Josette.

Why was he suddenly eager as hell to spend the evening with the gorgeous brunette? He was here for a wedding and a weekend of festivities.

Not a Mardi Gras fling, no matter how tempting the opportunity.

Now he only had to convince himself to buy that.

ADDISON RAN INTO three different groups of friends and family as they headed toward the elevator at the far end of the lobby. Each chance meeting required a conversation about the upcoming wedding. Josette tried to concentrate on everyone she was introduced to but doubted seriously she'd remember half of their names if she ran into them again.

Finally, they reached their suite and Addison inserted the key and pushed the door open, holding it for Josette to enter first.

Josette turned 360 degrees to take in the full effect of the opulent accommodations. The Princess Suite was worthy of its name. The corner unit was super plush with huge glass sliding doors that opened onto a balcony facing the very lively Bourbon Street.

The inside sitting area held a large sofa and two leather chairs that faced a big-screen TV. A bowl of fresh fruit graced a round coffee table. A bouquet of purple and gold blossoms rested on a lamp table between the two chairs. Framed pictures of French Quarter scenes decorated the walls.

An open door a few feet behind the sofa led to an elegant bedroom with a king-size bed and a large-screen TV. It also opened onto a balcony.

Josette dropped her handbag onto the coffee table. "So, this is how the rich and famous live."

"You know far more about that than I, Miss Fame and Fortune."

Addison's facial expression changed immediately, and it was clear she was sorry she'd made any reference to Isadora that might upset Josette.

"I'm sorry, Josette. I know you don't need a constant reminder of Isadora."

"No, but please don't worry about offending me with every casual comment." She gave her friend a hug, then stepped back. "I can't believe your dad's footing the bill for this suite. I remember weekends at your house. I always loved being around your parents."

"This whole French Quarter wedding was Dad's idea," Addison said. "He loves Mardi Gras and most every other New Orleans festival. Besides, this is probably still far cheaper than the destination wedding in Italy my mother thought we should have."

"Which did you prefer?"

"A compromise. A wedding in the French Quarter with all our friends and family and a month's honeymoon in Italy. We're all thrilled."

Josette settled into one of the leather chairs. "Is Bart okay with all the hoopla?"

"I think he's a little overwhelmed at times, but he

says anything I want works for him. He's a living doll that way."

"He's clearly mad about you."

"I feel the same about him." Addison stepped out of her black pumps and sat down on the sofa. "What did you think about Keenan or did you have time to form an opinion?"

"Not really." She should probably leave it at that, but it would just put off the inevitable. She knew her friend too well to think that would put an end to the questions. Besides, she had a question of her own. "Why didn't you mention earlier that Keenan and I would be on the same flight?"

Addison shrugged. "Too much on my mind, I guess."

Josette wasn't buying it. "Are you sure it wasn't because you were afraid I'd get bent out of shape because he's FBI? You know how aggravated I was with their initial investigation."

"That, too. I remember how angry you got when they started questioning you so persistently."

"Persistently…" She leaned forward. "And accusingly, as if they thought I was hiding something."

"And we all knew you weren't," said Addison. "But I admit I thought it would be better if you met Keenan before you knew he was FBI. Bart is certain the two of you are going to hit it off."

"Whether or not I liked Keenan, I'd do everything possible to make your wedding special."

Addison reached for her friend's hand and squeezed it. "I know. I shouldn't have worried. I wouldn't be surprised if he and Bart are discussing that right now. Bart insisted it was better to get everything out up front since it was bound to come up sooner or later."

"I agree."

She sat back and looked at Josette. "You hold up so well, but I know you must be worried about your mother."

"Of course, I am. I can't remember a time in my life when I wasn't worried about her. But she thrives on the excitement and popularity that goes with being a superstar—except when she decides she hates it."

If only it were that innocuous, she thought. She put on a brave face for her friend, but inside she was anything but. The longer her mother was gone, the more convinced she became that this was not one of Isadora's infamous disappearing acts. It just might be murder.

But Addison was getting married. Josette wouldn't burden her friend with that speculation.

"Surely one weekend without Mom's special blend of drama isn't too much to ask, right?" She said it off-handedly, despite the tightening in her belly.

"I'm just so glad you could make it. Nothing would have been the same without you here."

The luggage arrived. Addison let the bellhop in and directed him to a closed door on the right side of the suite. A second, slightly smaller, but totally fabulous bedroom and en suite bathroom, came into view.

"Your abode awaits," Addison said. "The adjoining door locks and the room also opens to the hallway if you need to come and go with more privacy."

"Thanks, but I suspect I'll hit the bed long before you do. I could never keep up with your partying lifestyle."

"I was thinking more about your convenience. You never know when romance will strike beneath the spell of a moonlit night in the French Quarter."

"Little chance of that. I'm horribly allergic to romance, especially ones that last over twenty-four hours."

Keenan's face came into her mind's eye and she could almost hear a voice in her head.

Never underestimate the FBI.

As soon as Keenan was alone in his room, he gave in to the overwhelming temptation. He turned on his computer and used his official FBI password to scan the available information on Isadora Guillory.

Due to her celebrity status, the FBI had been called into the case almost immediately after her disappearance. The NOPD had gathered little evidence of foul play but couldn't rule it out.

Rumors ran wild—everything from a rendezvous with a wealthy foreign lover to her going into protective custody after cooperating with the CIA to arrest the leader of an infamous drug cartel.

The latter was the backbone of a plot that had recently played out on her hit show, *The Winds of Scandal*. It appeared some of her more avid fans confused the real Isadora Guillory with the character she played on the show. Jill Hawthorne, a rich heiress who was constantly in danger.

A year ago, the FBI had put a team of their best agents on the case, including Dwayne Evans. Dwayne was a friend of Keenan but they'd both been so busy this past year, they hadn't talked often. Though Dwayne no longer was assigned the Guillory case, Keenan hadn't realized he had been involved at any stage.

The information indicated there had been dozens of reported sightings during the first few weeks of the investigation. The most credible included a service station in Little Rock, a motel near the Mexican border and a grocery store in Canada. None had panned out.

The little evidence they'd gathered over time diverged like roots of one of the ancient oak trees along the famed St. Charles Avenue in uptown New Orleans. One of the most promising suspects was a stalker who believed Isadora was his soul mate. He'd claimed he would kill her if he saw her with another man.

Unfortunately, the lunatic had an ironclad alibi for the week Isadora disappeared. He'd been in jail on a DWI charge at the time. He was currently doing time for a stalker case in Dallas. Keenan figured he'd switched soul mates.

The money trail also went nowhere. Though she'd withdrawn a large sum from a New Orleans bank days before her disappearance, there had been no other withdrawals from any of her other numerous accounts in more different countries than most people could name.

Three months ago, with no significant breakthroughs, the FBI and the NOPD reduced the priority level of the investigation. Needless to say, in a case this famous, it hadn't and wouldn't be dropped completely until it was solved.

This was far different from any case Keenan had been on before. It would be fascinating to explore the psyche of a woman whose life seemed like an adult version of hide-and-seek.

But no psych evaluation for him. He was only there for the wedding, he told himself as he powered down his laptop.

"I'M STUFFED," Josette said as she picked up her white linen napkin to wipe her mouth. "I don't think I've ever had better softshell crab."

"And I forget from one time to the next just how good the barbecued shrimp are here," Keenan said. "I didn't leave a bite and that was after the oysters on the half shell we had with cocktails."

"I figured if the wedding invitation wasn't enough to lure you down here, the food would be," Bart said. "But we're just getting started. Wedding's not until Monday evening."

Addison pushed her plate of half-eaten fillet of fish toward her fiancé. "Go ahead, pig out. I'll watch. If I gain one ounce, someone's going to have to squeeze me into my wedding dress."

"Josette will have to be assigned with that task," Bart quipped. "My job will be getting you out of it."

The waiter stopped by their dinner table and began

to fill their wine goblets with the remainder of their second bottle of Riesling.

"No more for me," Josette said. "I'm a lightweight."

"Nothing wrong with that," the waiter said. "How about the rest of you? Shall I uncork another bottle?"

They all agreed they'd had enough—for now.

"Are you locals or in town for Mardi Gras?" the waiter asked.

"Some of both," Keenan said. "Two locals, two visitors. I'm one of the latter and here to eat and drink my way to Fat Tuesday. Best seafood north of the Gulf."

"You're right about that," the waiter agreed. "But be careful out there. The drunker the revelers get, the wilder they get. Of course, if you ever want to get a little crazy, this is your chance. Anything goes at Mardi Gras, or 'bout near it."

"I'll keep them in line," Addison said.

"Yeah, like if temptation offered itself, you won't be the ringleader," Bart said.

"And that's why you love me."

"One of the many reasons."

Bart took care of the bill at his insistence. On Whelan Landry's tab, he assured them. Addison's dad really had insisted on taking care of all expenses.

When they hit the streets again, the pedestrians making their way down Royal Street became a suffocating crush of humanity. Couples and groups crowded the pavement, most with to-go cups in hand and multiple strings of Mardi Gras beads around their necks.

Addison quickly joined in the fun, interacting with the people lining the balconies who called to her to lift her blouse and earn some beads. She didn't comply but she was so cute when she flipped that long blond hair and flashed her come-hither look, most of the guys dropped beads into her hands anyway.

"You have that down to a fine art," Keenan said.

She smiled. "Comes from years of going to parades and begging for throws."

"For beaded necklaces you can buy by the dozens for a few dollars," Bart added.

"The thrill is in the catch," Addison reminded him as she placed another string of beads around her neck.

Josette ignored the chanting directed her way. She had just enough claustrophobia that being jam-packed into a yelling throng of people made it difficult to breathe. The nosebleed heels that had been great with her favorite black dress in the restaurant now had her feet complaining.

"A street performer must really be putting on a show down there," Bart said, pointing to the next block where a group of people in the middle of the street totally gridlocked movement.

Bart took Addison's hand. She grabbed Josette's hand as did Keenan and they stepped over the curb and retreated to a souvenir storefront. Thankfully, there was a bit of breathing room there.

"I've seen that same show a few dozen times before," Bart joked. "Same act, different performers. You guys watch while I duck into this shop. I'll only be a minute."

Addison took a phone call, though Josette couldn't imagine how she could hear over the noisy din. Josette went back to people watching.

Somehow her thoughts went back to her mother despite her attempts to get past them.

Her mother had been here in the French Quarter on a night that was almost surely as alive as this. No one loved a party more than Isadora and she was always the focus of everyone's attention, especially the men.

Josette could imagine her mother here, laughing, no doubt waving and throwing kisses to everyone.

For her own safety, she'd likely have been on a balcony with her bodyguards nearby. Hordes of people would have recognized her and jammed the streets while she threw trinkets and kisses to everyone.

Suddenly the images in Josette's mind merged with reality. A woman was standing on a nearby balcony with her back to the crowd. Luminous, slightly wild auburn curls cascading past her slender shoulders. Her dress was the color of sapphires, sequined, stretchy, stopping midthigh, hugging her perfect body. Josette's heart rate soared and her skin flushed. Could it be? Was—

And then the woman turned toward the crowd below and Josette's spirits plunged. It wasn't Isadora, not that she'd really thought it would be.

Keenan wrapped his arm around her waist to steady her. "You're trembling. What's wrong?"

"Just a little wooziness. Too many people in too little space, I guess."

"I get that. I'll walk you back to the hotel if you want."

"Thanks, but I can go it alone. No use for you to miss the party."

"My leg insists otherwise."

Addison put her phone away. "What's this about going back to the hotel? Are you not feeling well, Josette?"

"Just got dizzy for a second. I think the wine and the smothering crowds got to me."

Bart rejoined them, a plastic bag in hand. "What's next? Shall we look for someplace with music or do you want to keep fighting the crowds?"

"Hate to be a party pooper, but I think I'll call it a night," Josette said. "We have a big day tomorrow."

"Why don't I walk you back to the hotel?" Bart said, then he turned to his friend and his fiancée. "And you two can party till you drop."

"With this leg, 'till I drop' might not be more than ten minutes," Keenan said. "I'll walk Josette back and you two go ahead. No use wasting a night of partying because of us."

Addison reached out and laid her hand on Bart's arm. "Actually, that was one of my cousins on the phone," she said. "She and her husband decided to drive in from Baton Rouge tonight instead of waiting until tomorrow morning. Luckily, someone canceled at the last minute, and they got a room at our hotel. I told her we'd hook up with them in the hotel lounge. She said they have some live music there that's not bad."

"Sounds like a winner to me," Bart said.

No one disagreed, though Josette still planned to go straight to her room and get a grip on her emotions.

As they neared the hotel, Bart handed Josette the plastic bag.

She peeked inside and discovered an assortment of brightly colored Mardi Gras beads.

"Those are for tossing off your balcony whenever the mood strikes," Bart said. "You never know when the celebration might bring out your wilder side."

"She has one," Addison warned. "Trust me on that."

Keenan grinned. "Sounds intriguing."

Josette removed one of the necklaces from the bag and slipped it around his neck. "Hate to disappoint you, but this is as crazy as I'll get tonight."

Keenan fingered his necklace. "Good. Otherwise I couldn't keep up with you. Now about tomorrow, Bart. Do I have to get up before noon?"

"I'll be running my personal wedding guest airport shuttle in the morning, but there's nothing on the calendar for you until we hook up with Moose and Lance for a late lunch," Bart said. "Probably two-ish. After that, we'll pick up the monkey suits."

"Two-ish. Now that I can handle."

"And for the females?" Josette asked.

"Sara and Beth will join us by noon," Addison explained. "Mother is hosting high tea for some of the family in town for the wedding, so we'll need to leave the hotel about 1:30 for that. A driver will pick us up. And then hopefully we can catch a nap before the evening's Mardi Gras ball."

"Which is black tie," Bart added. "Not the navy blue tuxes we'll wear for the wedding. So, we pick up two tuxes each."

"No wonder you need a wedding planner," Keenan said. "Whatever happened to flying to Vegas and getting married by an Elvis impersonator?"

"That was my first choice," Bart quipped good-naturedly.

Addison wrapped her hands around Bart's arm and looked up at him, batting her eyes playfully. "Who needs Elvis when we have you gorgeous guys?" Addison said. Her smile turned to a frown when she turned back to Josette.

"About the ball, I hope it doesn't make you uncomfortable, Josette."

Josette didn't need the reminder. Ever since Addison had mentioned the Mardi Gras ball, she'd felt on edge, clammy, with a persistent pain in her chest. Her mother had attended one of the many balls the night she went missing.

It was almost as if she was re-creating her mother's last visit to New Orleans. She would have done anything in her power to avoid this but she could never not be here for her best friend.

"I know how difficult this is for you, staying at the same hotel and now going to one of the balls," Addison said, no doubt sensing her uneasiness. "You know the balls are major events for the krewes and Dad was naturally invited to several. He chose the one that issued engraved requests not only for him and Mother, but for the entire wedding party. You know Dad. He's always in high demand on the Mardi Gras circuit."

That didn't surprise Josette. He was one of the most well-known philanthropists in the city.

Addison took her hand. "If it's too much for you, you can pass on the ball."

"I'll be fine," she assured Addison. She wouldn't back out and be rude to Whelan Landry.

Once they reached the hotel, she and Keenan said their goodbyes to Addison and Bart at the door to the hotel bar and started down the hallway toward the elevators. Josette couldn't wait to get to the Princess Suite, alone. She wanted nothing more than to take a shower and wash away the morbid thoughts and fears that were dripping over her. She was concentrating so hard at just putting one foot in front of the other that she didn't see the throng of people heading toward her, till a flash of bright light had her looking up. A pack of about a dozen men and women pushed into her personal space. Mics were thrust in her face. Questions were hurled at her like darts.

"Have you heard from your mother?"

"Is Isadora alive?"

"Is Isadora coming back to *The Winds of Scandal*?"

"Is Isadora in protective custody?"

She tried to step back from the throng and nearly stumbled. It was the final question that almost had her falling to the ground.

"Is there any truth to the rumor that Isadora is turning up for Mardi Gras?"

What? Her mother was coming to New Orleans in a few days? She scanned the crowd for the reporter, wanting to get more information, but the camera flashes came closer, nearly blinding her. The lobby felt as if it were spinning and her heart felt as if it would beat out of her chest. Out of the corner of her eye she spotted a dark figure as it bolted through the crowd of onlookers, plowing straight into her and pushing her back into the wall. With the force, her head slammed back and just as everything around her was about to go black, Keenan cut a swath through the jungle of photographers and rubberneckers and grabbed her. His strong arms wrapped around her; they were all that kept her from falling to the floor in a heap.

"Josette," he called. "Are you all right?" He wasted no time for her reply. He picked her up and strode toward the elevators.

Hotel workers stepped in to help control the crowd, commanding the guests disperse and the reporters leave.

By the time they reached the elevators, a couple of hotel workers and an armed security guard were holding the door for them. She could tell Keenan was reluctant to put her down, but she insisted, holding on to the bar along the wall for support. The guard rode with them to the second floor.

Two more uniformed men were waiting there.

"Sorry for the inconvenience," the armed guard apologized. "The hotel does its best to ensure everyone's safety and privacy on weekends like this, but the paparazzi show no respect. If you plan to go out again tonight, alert hotel security first. We'll take care of you."

"Thanks," she said. "I will, but I plan to stay in my room for the evening, maybe for the whole weekend if that's going to be waiting for me every time I step into the lobby."

"I'll walk you to your room," one of the security detail offered. "Don't let those sharks keep you from enjoying Mardi Gras. There's plenty of uniformed and plainclothes officers on the streets tonight and they'll be there throughout Fat Tuesday. Trouble starts and they'll be on it in seconds."

"Good to know," Keenan said. "Thanks again for the quick work tonight."

Seconds later, at her door, Josette slipped her magnetic key into the slot. She stepped inside but left the door open. Apparently, taking that as an invitation, Keenan followed her inside.

The guard left and she closed the door and set the dead bolt.

Keenan ushered her into the living room. "You never did answer me. Are you okay?"

She fingered the back of her head, checking her hand for blood. Seeing none, she nodded. "I'm fine. Thanks to you, probably. Any idea who knocked me down?"

He shook his head. "Didn't see anything until I heard your head hit the wall. But by then, whoever it was must have disappeared into the crowd."

"Probably an overeager paparazzo." Who else would it be? Why would anyone want to harm her?

"Well, I must admit that was a little more excitement than I was expecting," Keenan said. "Do you get that kind of reception often?"

"Too often lately. But they're only interested in my mother. I'm sure you know that I'm the daughter of the famous Isadora Guillory."

"I'm guessing most everyone in the hotel has figured that out by now," he agreed. "But yes, I already knew."

"I'm sure you did. You are FBI, after all." What was wrong with her? The man had gotten her away from the crowd of reporters. Why was she taking a sharp tone with him?

"What's that supposed to mean?" he asked her.

"Come on, Keenan. I know you're looking to get information from me about my mother's disappearance. Just in a much nicer way than those paparazzi downstairs. For that I'm grateful, at least." She sat down on the sofa and peered up at him. "Do you want me to tell you the same thing I told all the other cops and agents who accused me of having something to do with my mother's disappearance?"

Keenan sat beside her. "Josette, it's not what you think. I'm not here in any official capacity. I'm on medical leave from the Bureau for my leg. Besides, I didn't even know who you were when I met you on the plane."

He sounded so sincere, she had to stare into his face to gauge his honesty. His dark hair was tousled, no doubt from how he'd swept through the crowd to rescue her, and his brown eyes held no hint of a lie.

What was wrong with her? This mystery surrounding her mother was making her paranoid. Keenan was telling the truth.

"How did you find out who I am? Bart told you?"

He shook his head. "The original tattletale was the man sitting by me on the airplane after you turned down my great company. Bart just confirmed it."

"It doesn't matter," she said. "It was bound to come out."

Her telephone rang and she reached into her purse for it. As expected, it was Addison.

"Are you okay?" her friend asked in a frantic tone. No doubt she'd heard about the scene in the lobby.

"Sorry for the sideshow, but I survived," Josette said.

"Where are you?" Addison asked.

"In our room, with the door locked."

"Thank goodness. I panicked there for a minute. Let me explain your catastrophe to my cousin and I'll be right up. You shouldn't be alone."

"I'm not alone. Keenan is here and I'm fine."

"Ah, you're with Keenan. Better watch yourself with him," she teased. "He's not only gorgeous but he was super impressive guiding you through the teeming fans and rabid reporters and photographers. The FBI to the rescue and all that jazz."

"Right, whatever 'all that jazz' means."

"Just that you're in good hands, so I'll stop worrying about you. I won't be out late. We're right downstairs in the lounge. Call if you need me."

"I won't. Need you, that is. Have fun."

There was a knock at the door by the time she finished the call with Addison.

"Hotel Security checking to see if Ms. Guillory needs anything."

Keenan got up and peered through the peephole.

"He's alone, has a security badge and no camera. And he's small enough I could take him," Keenan said, no doubt trying to keep the moment as light as possible.

"Then ready those muscles and open the door," Josette retorted.

Keenan did and Josette walked over to assure the man she was safe and needed nothing. When the guard left, she leaned against the door, her breathing steadying.

"I'm sorry I pulled you into this, Keenan."

"I don't recall you doing any pulling, and whatever you feel, don't let it be regret. It's the first time I've felt useful since I was awarded my few minutes of glory before I graduated to rehab."

"Rehab or not, you handled that situation like a pro."

"Thank you, ma'am. You were tough out there yourself. I thought for a minute you were going to take the supersize camera away from that skinny, loudmouthed photographer and shove it— Well, luckily, he backed away before we found out where you'd shove it."

"And if I had shoved it anywhere, he would have sued me. That's the game. They push you over the edge and then yell assault and threaten lawsuits. Not all of them, of course. Just the worst ones—according to Mother."

She kicked off the stiletto heels that had been a huge disadvantage in outrunning the persistent reporters. The tight skirt on her favorite black dress hadn't helped, either.

"Would you like company for a while?" Keenan asked. "I'm not pushing for you to keep me around. You can say no if you don't feel like talking and I'll scoot down the hall to my own room."

This wasn't the flirty tone he'd used on the plane. He sounded serious now. Concern etched his hazel eyes.

Unexpected warmth zinged through her. The truth was she wanted him to stay for reasons she didn't want to examine.

Addison was right. Gorgeous and protective were hard traits to ignore in a man.

Chapter Four

Keenan checked out the suite while Josette excused herself to change into something more comfortable. Hopefully that didn't mean more seductive, as if anything short of naked could be more seductive than the black dress she was wearing now. It would be embarrassing if he started to drool.

Bottles of expensive whiskey, vodkas, liqueurs and wine sat on a shelf next to a filled ice bucket. The booze looked tempting, but he decided to pass. Too much going on this weekend to start with a hangover or bad judgment.

He filled two glasses with water and took them onto the balcony. Music blared from a bar just down the block. High-pitched voices and laughter were practically deafening.

Apparently, Mardi Gras hadn't changed much since the last time Keenan was here for Mardi Gras and that was back when he was in college. Anything goes. Best party to be found. The freshman battle cry.

He didn't hear Josette approach until she was standing at his elbow. Awareness knocked around inside him as he turned toward her.

At least she'd tried not to send his lust factor sky-rocketing. She'd gone for the girl-next-door look with a loose-fitting pale yellow sweater over black leggings. It didn't help. She still looked good enough to get a rise out of him.

He handed her a glass. "It's only water but I can make you a real drink if you'd like."

"Water is exactly what I need." She clinked her glass with his. "Do you want some beads to tempt the women to show you what they've got?"

A siren screamed in the distance. She repeated the question twice before he could hear her.

"No," he finally answered. "I've had all the excitement I can handle just from the view walking back to the hotel. That is, unless you're looking for beads."

"No thanks. Got a bag full. How about we go back inside so we can hear each other speak," she suggested. "Besides, no use to let all that Princess Suite extravagance go to waste."

"I'll second that."

Once back inside, Keenan closed the sliding glass doors behind them. Josette settled into one of the leather chairs. She stepped out of a pair of fuzzy black slippers and tucked her feet into the chair with her.

"Feel free to kick off your shoes and stretch your wounded leg out on the sofa," Josette offered.

"Thanks." He took her up on the offer, then took a deep breath and exhaled slowly as the ache in his left thigh eased. The pain was only a fraction as bad as it had been for the first month after he'd taken shrapnel in the explosion, but long days like this still took their toll.

"Tell me about the limp," she said, "or would you rather not talk about it?"

"I never like to talk about weaknesses. I prefer to pretend I can master anything. But the explosion got my attention."

"It sounds as if you didn't know what was coming."

"Oh, we knew, all right. We just didn't know when, where and how bad. We thought we did. We misjudged, leading us to overlook some key factors, any of which could have been deadly to all or any of us."

Josette winced. "And yet I get the impression that you'll sign right up for the next dangerous mission."

Keenan lightly massaged his left calf. "Doesn't sound too bright, does it? But yes, you're right, only this time I'll be better at it than I was before. So will every guy on my team."

"You're either extremely dedicated, Keenan, or you enjoy living on the edge."

"A little of both. That's the truth most days." He lowered his foot to the floor and angled himself toward her. "Right now, I'm more worried about that paparazzi group that I thought was going to eat you alive. Are they always so aggressive?"

"Pretty much."

She worried the hem of her sweater—a nervous tic, he guessed. Then she looked up and her eyes met his. "Look, Keenan, about before… I don't know how familiar you are with my mother's disappearance," she said, "but the FBI participated in the original investigation. They can be very aggressive, too. They questioned me thoroughly, several times, in fact—even though I assured them I was not involved in her disappearance and I could prove it. I half expected them to arrest me every time they showed up."

"That doesn't mean they suspected you of any wrongdoing," Keenan said. "They go at a case from every angle."

"Maybe, but they hit a couple of the angles especially hard."

"It was a high-profile case, so they would have been determined not to overlook any clues."

"I wish they had found some clues. Getting away from everyone and everything seems to be Mother's goal when she takes one of her time-outs to regroup her life."

"Then you weren't shocked when you heard she was missing?"

"Even less surprised than on previous occasions. This time she'd called me a couple of weeks before to lament her current dissatisfaction with the producers and directors of her TV show."

"But she didn't say she was leaving or where she might be heading?" Kennan asked.

"No. That's not her style." Her voice was uneven, a bit raspy when she continued. He caught the shimmer of tears in her eyes. "But I haven't heard from her since she disappeared. She usually calls me at least once to make sure I'm okay. Nothing this time."

"Awfully hard to understand how a woman with

millions of ardent fans could vanish so completely whenever she chooses," Keenan said. "But then, some criminals stay on the Most Wanted list for decades, living in plain sight for the most part."

"That's not particularly comforting," she said and he immediately regretted his statement. She needed reassurance, not a dose of reality. Before he could offer her any comfort, she cleared her throat and sat up straighter. "Enough talk about my mother. No use getting bogged down with things I can't change."

Her voice belied the concern her words were trying to hide. "Sometimes talking offers a new prospective on things," he suggested.

"Is that direct from the FBI manual?"

"No. Just my own take on prospects."

They sat in silence for a few minutes. She didn't ask him to leave, so he figured she wasn't ready to be alone. Being here for Mardi Gras was undoubtedly bringing all her concerns about Isadora to the surface.

And the FBI in him made him hate to let the mystery go.

"What was it like growing up with such a famous mother?"

JOSETTE WRAPPED HER arms around her chest, pulling inside herself as she always did when dealing with family issues. She'd been asked that same question or some form of it hundreds of times before, usually by some reporter looking for dirt or intrigue.

She'd never dissed her mother even on days she'd wanted to. She wouldn't start now, but for some inexplicable reason, she found herself wanting to open up to this man she'd met only hours ago. A man she'd likely never see again after this weekend.

Perhaps that's what made sharing with him feel nonthreatening.

"Do you want to hear the good parts or the bad parts?" she asked. "Because there were plenty of both."

"You make that call."

Moments slipped by as Josette let the memories haunt her mind. She rearranged herself in her chair. "Are you sure you want to go there tonight?"

"Yes, unless you don't feel up to it."

Surprisingly, she did.

"I've given it lots of thought and analysis over the years. The best description of life with the infamous Isadora Guillory that I can come up with is its similarity to a recurring dream I had growing up."

She met Keenan's eyes and something in their piercing depth made her feel safe enough to reveal more.

"I'm on a roller coaster, squealing with delight. I can see my mother on the ground waving and smiling and throwing me kisses. Suddenly, Mother's excitement turns to a look of panic. That's when I realize my security bar isn't locked and we're about to take a loop that will send me hurtling into space."

Josette closed her eyes momentarily as the familiar memory crept from the deeper grottos of her mind.

His gaze burning into hers, he leaned forward, his elbows on his knees. "What happens then?"

"I wake up. That was life with Mother. Excitement

one minute, sliding into uncertainty the next. Never knowing exactly what the future would hold."

"Where's your dad while you're alone on the roller coaster?"

"He's never there. It wouldn't happen if he were there. He'd be on the roller coaster with me, making sure I was buckled in and keeping me safe."

"Glad for good old Dad," Keenan said.

"Mother left the bayou for New York to become a star when I was three, so I only have very few early memories of her living with us, though she did visit several times over the years.

"I was ten when she decided that I should move to New York to live with her and a series of nannies and housekeepers."

"What prompted her to move to New York the first time when you were just a preschooler?"

"A production crew came into our area to film a movie. Mother got a job as an extra that turned into a speaking part. She stunned the producer as she does everyone with her beauty and talent. She did one TV series after another until she hit the big time with *The Winds of Scandal*."

"And a career she obviously runs away from on occasion," Keenan added.

"True. I know I'm biased, but Mom is the most beautiful woman I've ever seen. She literally sparkles. People look at her and instantly fall in love. Sometimes, she falls in love right back, but with her it never lasts long. I think she's always been in love with my father on some level—they never divorced, you see. But I guess she craves the fame and popularity far more."

"Does he still love her?"

"In his way, I think, but as he always says, he's a simple shrimper. His life is on the bayou. Mother was born to be a star."

Josette's phone rang. She took it from the table beside her and checked the caller ID. "Ah, it's Dad. Guess he sensed we were talking about him."

"I'll wait on the balcony and give you some privacy," Keenan offered.

"That's okay. Stay here. I'll take the call in my bedroom.

"Hi, Dad," she answered as she stepped into her bedroom, closing the door behind her. "It's late for you to be calling. Is something wrong?"

"That's what I'm wondering," Antoine said. "Why are you in New Orleans for Mardi Gras? And why didn't you tell me you were coming?"

He sounded agitated and she did her best to calm him down. "No reason, Dad. I'm here just for a few days. I—"

"Don't lie to me, Josette," he barked into her ear. "I know something is up. I heard the rumors about Isadora. Everyone's heard them. Even here in Alligator Cove. If you know something about your mother, you must tell me."

Now she knew why he sounded frantic. The paparazzo's question about Isadora reappearing at Mardi Gras had thrown her, too. It might be just the kind of publicity stunt her mother would pull, but could they believe anything so fantastical? "Dad, listen to me. You remember Addison Landry, my roommate at LSU? She's getting married Monday night in the French Quarter and I'm here to be her maid of honor."

"Why didn't you tell me instead of trying to keep it a secret?"

"My mistake." Trying to keep anything from Antoine had always been a mistake, especially if it involved Isadora. "How did you find out I was in New Orleans?"

"Harley Broussard. He said he only saw you in passing."

"Interesting, since he pretended not to see me at all and then apparently couldn't wait to tell you."

"That's probably for the best." He hesitated and his voice dropped to a lower octave when he starting speaking again. "Look, Josette, I didn't plan to tell you until the decision had been put into effect, but there's no reason not to give you the details now. The decision is made."

"What decision? You sound so serious you're starting to make me nervous."

"Don't be. I've thought this through. I'm selling the shrimp boat."

Her breath came fast and quick. "You're selling the *Lady Isadora*? Did I hear that right?"

"You heard right."

"Why would you sell it? The boat is practically new. Mom bought it for you when the other boat started showing its age. It's a beautiful boat."

He hesitated a moment before responding. "I know this is going to take you by surprise but I'm giving up shrimping, at least for now."

"You're not ill, are you?"

"My health is perfect."

"Is this Lorraine's idea? Does she want you to sell the boat just because Mom gave it to you?" There was no love lost between Isadora and her father's lady friend.

"Lorraine does not run my life. Neither does your mother."

No way was that true. Everything in her dad's life had always had something to do with Isadora. Maybe this time she really had broken Antoine's heart, but Josette couldn't just stand by and watch him throw his life away.

"Look, Dad. I'm not sure how I'll finagle it, but I'll find a way to get down to you first thing in the morning. Promise me you won't make any final decision until we've talked in person."

"I've already made the decision. Your coming down here is totally unnecessary. Just stay put and *laissez les bons temps rouler.* I'll call you soon."

He broke the connection before she could ask any more questions. Anxiety skated along her nerve endings.

She struggled without success to make sense of her father's news before rejoining Keenan in the living area. She failed.

Keenan was pacing the room as if he were past ready to leave.

"Is everything okay?" he asked.

"I'm not sure. Dad was talking out of his head. I need to rent a car and drive down to see him first thing tomorrow morning. Otherwise, I'll just worry when I should be celebrating the wedding."

"Makes sense," Keenan agreed. "Tell you what. I have an offer too good to refuse."

"Let's hear it."

"I'll arrange for a car and drive you to see your father. You buy breakfast."

"Why on earth would you do that?"

"What can I say? I've got a craving to breathe some bayou air."

KEENAN WOULD HAVE sworn he'd just dropped off to sleep when his alarm went off at six. He and Josette would have to get an early start if they were going to make it back from her dad's in time for the afternoon's planned activities.

They'd agreed to meet in the hotel lobby at seven. Fortunately, Keenan had the car lined up. He'd located Bart in the lounge downing tequila shots when Keenan left Josette last night. Without hesitation, Bart had handed him the valet ticket to his BMW.

He'd assured Keenan he would just borrow one of his future father-in-law's cars for the day. Evidently, Whelan Landry had several vehicles at his command.

Keenan grabbed a quick shower and dressed in a pair of jeans and a short-sleeve T-shirt.

The high today was supposed to get up to the mid-seventies. Perfect early March weather for all the parades. Once dressed, he had one job to do before he went down to meet Josette. He grabbed a hotel pen and writing pad, ready to take a few quick notes. A habit he couldn't break.

Dwayne's number was in his phone contacts. They'd made friends a few years ago, after a case they'd worked together before Keenan had moved to the terrorist division.

Dwayne grunted and grumbled his hello. "Do you know what time it is, buddy?"

"Dawn outside. Must be morning."

"It's also Saturday and I have the day off. But now that I'm half-awake, this better be good." His colleague's mumbling turned clearer. Typical agent behavior. Like doctors, they were frequently woken up in the middle of the night and needed to be coherent quickly.

"Could be. Do you remember Isadora Guillory?"

"Sure. The missing TV star. I was on that case for a while. No way to forget that one. Don't tell me you're running in her circles now."

"Not so much running as limping and not so much *her* circles but her daughter's."

"Getting better all the time. When you say her daughter, you're talking about the gorgeous heiress Josette Guillory?"

"Yes. Nothing to do with the FBI. We're in a wedding together."

"I assume you're not the groom."

Keenan let out a laugh. "No. Just playing a bit role.

I'm down here in NOLA. Lots of drinking, eating and throwing beads together."

"You lucky dog. Did you call me just to brag?"

"A little, maybe. More to pick your brain."

He heard shuffling and figured Dwayne was sitting up in bed or maybe had gotten up entirely. "Last I heard Isadora was wearing her invisibility cloak. Did she ever show up?"

"Not yet."

"With the kind of money she has scattered in banks all around the globe, she could be anywhere, with anyone on the planet."

That was the problem, Keenan thought to himself. "All that money legal?" he asked.

"We never proved otherwise, at least not back when I was on the case. No bank fraud. No money laundering. No tax evasion. The woman loves shopping and rich men, not necessarily in that order."

Keenan cut to the chase, the reason he was reaching out to his old friend. "What about motives for abducting or killing her?"

"You name it. Filthy lucre, revenge, betrayal, lust, jealousy, envy. Her life was more byzantine than any work of fiction I've ever read. The Bureau never found any sign of foul play at the time."

"Might be time to give that a second look," Keenan said.

"Might be."

Keenan filled him on what little he knew, including the rumor that the elusive Isadora Guillory was set to reappear on Mardi Gras. From the news feed on his phone, the story had been picked up by several outlets, though it had been credited only to "an unnamed source."

"I have to go now, but if you get a chance to review the case and run across anything you think I'd find interesting, give me a call, will you?"

"Do I need to remind you that you're not officially on this case or any other at the moment?"

"I know that all too well. I'm just a concerned friend with absolutely no authority—unless, of course, the Bureau or the local police department invites me in."

Keenan also knew he was in this way too deep to just walk away now—with or without that authority. Josette was definitely getting under his skin.

Chapter Five

Josette stopped at the hotel coffee shop and picked up tall coffees, disposable cups of ice water, blueberry scones and two bright yellow bananas. She reached the hotel lobby at 6:55 a.m.

Keenan was waiting, his hair slightly mussed, his face cleanly shaved and showing no signs that he already regretted giving up half his day to chauffeur her around.

"You said breakfast," she said, holding up the cardboard carrier that supported the coffees and waters. "You didn't specify what kind of breakfast."

"As long as it includes coffee, I'm good with it."

"I hope you like it black. I forgot cream or sweeteners."

"I always take my coffee black and I like my iced tea and women sweet."

She wasn't sure she'd fit into that "sweet" category. Not after her behavior last night. She hoped he'd forgiven her for accusing him of an ulterior motive. She smiled at him. "Then we'd best stick to coffee. Do we have a car or are we hitchhiking?"

"That was the only-if-all-else-fails option," Keenan teased. "Luckily, Bart lent us his car. It's waiting and ready to go. You do know how to get to your dad's house, right?"

"In my sleep. Traffic shouldn't be too bad through Metairie and Kenner this early, but the later it gets, the worse the backups. Some streets near or on the parade routes get blocked completely, making it nearly impossible to get across town. This is a city-wide party."

"Then let's get going." Keenan relieved her of the coffee carrier as they started toward the revolving doors. Once outside, the doorman led them to the car, which was parked a few feet away. Keenan had already made arrangements with the valet to bring the car around. He handed Keenan the key.

Streets that had been overrun with loud revelers the night before were deserted this morning. The quiet was strangely eerie.

"How long is the drive?" Keenan asked, as he fit their drinks into holders on the console.

"Depends on the traffic, but we should be able to make it back in time for today's activities."

Josette adjusted her seat belt. "Once we get there, you'll feel like you've entered a different world, an even more humid one with bayous that spread and braid the land like icing on a cinnamon roll. You'll fight off swarms of mosquitoes and be entertained by noisy, colorful birds and perhaps an alligator or two. But then, going to LSU, you must have made more than a few trips into the swamp."

He shook his head as he sipped his coffee, keeping his eyes on the road. "Wasn't my favorite pastime."

"Then you'd best be careful. You know what they say, wander off too far into one of the swamps and you may never come out." She said it in her best mock movie-narrator voice, deep and tremulous. It was intended as a joke, but for some reason, she felt a chill that had nothing to do with the air-conditioning blowing into the car to mitigate the rising morning humidity.

"I think I saw that movie," Keenan said, going along with the joke. "Quicksand, man-eating gators and hundred-foot-long snakes."

"Fortunately, the reptiles move slowly this time of year. You may not spot an alligator or a snake."

He sent her an exaggerated sad face. "Oh, and I was so looking forward to making friends with a cute little gator."

"Don't knock it. A lot of people make a good living providing swamp tours for tourists and they guarantee seeing an alligator or two. Sometimes the guide will even bring a baby gator onto the boat and let the guests hold it. It's quite an experience—at least for the tourists."

"I'll take your word for it."

Keenan deftly navigated the narrow French Quarter streets. Once they reached the interstate, Josette sipped her coffee and settled into the ride as her thoughts drifted back to her father's news.

Keenan made no attempt at casual conversation and Josette didn't break the silence until they crossed the Mississippi River at Interstate 610. By then Keenan had finished his scone and a banana. Josette stuck with her black coffee for now. She wasn't big on breakfast even on a good day. And she certainly wouldn't classify this as one. Anticipating the meeting with her father had put her on edge. What was going on with him that made him determined to sell his shrimp boat?

"I feel terrible that you're missing out on time with the guys," Josette said, "but I really appreciate the company."

"I'm a guy. We can only take so much organized fun unless there's some kind of ball involved. Besides, there's still two days of fun and games before the wedding."

"Good point. How did Bart take the idea of your running out on him?"

"Great. He didn't hesitate to suggest I take his car. If anything, he seemed glad I was going with you, even reminded me what a rough year you've had."

"Still, I owe you one."

"If you insist, I'm sure I can think of some way you can repay me."

"I'll just bet you can." Would he ask her for a kiss? Not that she'd be opposed to it. She wondered what it'd be like to kiss Keenan. Truthfully, she'd been wondering about it since she'd met him on the plane. The stubble from last night was gone and she caught a dimple in his cheek as he flashed her a mischievous smile. Was that the faint hint of a scar on his chin? A remnant of his last terrorism task force mission perhaps? When all this with her dad and mom was over, she'd have to ask him.

"I'm actually glad to have you along for company," Josette admitted, "even if you didn't give me a lot of choice."

"That's another problem with us FBI guys. Even when we're not in charge, we think we are."

"I thought that went with being a man."

He barked out a laugh. "Touché." He was silent for a moment, then, "This is probably a good time to admit that I talked to one of my colleagues at the Bureau this morning."

"Doing a little research on me?" This time her tone wasn't accusatory, but rather playful.

"Just trying to get the whole picture clear in my mind. If nothing else, I might be able to steer you toward someone who can help track down your mother."

"You mean like a private detective?"

"That's one possibility."

"I hired a team of them. They were less help than the police and the FBI put together. Mostly they traveled to great vacation spots around the world on my dime—or rather several thousand dollars—with the excuse that they had reports of Mother being spotted there."

"Nice job if you can get it."

"I fired them at Christmas. Their concluding report consisted of basically nothing. I understand the detectives hired by *The Winds of Scandal* haven't been any more successful. What did you learn from your FBI contact?"

"Mostly what I'd already heard from you or read on the internet. But on the bright side, my colleague agrees that your mother's history suggests she could easily be safe and choosing to live in secret as she's done several times before."

The news should have put her more at ease but she just couldn't shake the dread that overtook her every time she thought of Isadora lately. "I wish I could believe that. It's just that this is the first time she's ever stayed gone so long and not called. She's even missed filming most of the upcoming season of *The Winds of Scandal*."

"What was the longest she went missing before this?"

"Seven months."

"Where had she been then?"

"Living with a prince from the Middle East. She raved about the experience but showed up a few weeks before filming for the next season's episodes got underway. She won an Emmy that year. Evidently, the added publicity paid off."

"What about her relationships at work?"

"She and her costar frequently feud about who should get the most screen time and money. That's all behind-the-scenes stuff. In public, they put on a show. The fans love thinking the on-screen chemistry between them is real."

"Anyone else besides—"

"Grant Gaines."

"Anyone else besides Grant Gaines that she clashes with?"

"There are occasional spats with the producer and the writers when her creative ideas differ from theirs, but it always blows over."

"What about her romantic entanglements? Was the prince completely out of the picture before she left this time?"

"Completely. There's always a steady stream of new men in her life. Don't get me wrong. I love my mother. I've never claimed to understand her but even when we're at odds, I always love her and I know she loves me—in her own unusual fashion."

Keenan reached across the seat and took her hand in his.

His touch felt like a lifeline, something steady to hold on to in a sea of the unknown.

But that's all it was, all it could be at this point, she told herself. They were still practically strangers and after the wedding on Monday evening, Keenan would likely be out of her life forever.

If there was one truth she'd learned from her mother, it was that relationships were tentative at best.

THEY DROVE MOSTLY in silence until they reached Bayou Lafourche. At that point Josette became talkative again, describing the bayou towns they passed, the houses sitting along the edge of the bayou as if it were a separate highway.

Shrimpers, airboats, pirogues and even groups of kayakers shared the slow-moving waterway with various creatures of the swamp. Keenan would love to come back and explore the area when there was more time. Josette would make a fabulous tour guide.

He might as well admit it, doing anything with Josette would be exciting. No doubt some of that was due to the fact that she was surrounded by mystery. And perhaps danger that sent out treacherous tendrils in every direction. Being an agent was in his blood and he'd forever be drawn to mystery and danger.

He couldn't ignore the risk of foul play associated with Isadora's disappearance. If she'd been killed and Josette got too close to the truth, the threat to her life would become harrowingly real.

That was something he couldn't forget.

Josette lowered her window a few inches. "I hope you don't mind, but I love the musky, pungent odors of the bayou and wetlands.

"I must have some of my mother in me. I like to visit this area but have no desire to move back here."

"So, you plan to stay in Nashville?"

"Unless I find a good reason not to. I'm totally into the country music scene, especially since I have a few very successful singers who love my designs."

"Impressive. Can you get me front-row tickets to one of their performances?"

"Maybe. Who would you like to see?"

"Anyone who could fill out your designs the way you did that black dress last night."

Her cheeks turned slightly red. God, she looked good in a blush. A twitch in his groin area reminded him to get his mind back on track.

"We're getting close to Alligator Cove," Josette finally said.

"Is that a town?"

"A small fishing village where my dad and a few other fishermen, especially shrimpers, live and work." She pointed out the window. "Look quickly across the bayou and you'll get a glimpse of what used to be my grandmother's house."

All he saw was a dilapidated cabin next to a cluster of cypress trees.

There was no traffic, so Keenan slowed and then stopped on the shoulder for a better look at the disintegrating structure. Most of the roof and all the windows were missing. The house leaned so far to the left that it looked as if it would cave into the bayou at the first strong gust of wind.

"It's hard to believe that was ever livable," Keenan said.

"It was, and not so long ago. Dad finally insisted Maumer move into a nursing home in Larose. Of course, the cabin was in much better shape then, thanks to Dad's constant attempts to repair it. The last hurricane finished it off, and he gave up."

"Your dad's roots must—"

"Look at the alligators!" Josette excitedly interrupted Keenan for a new update. "On the move, at the edge of the bayou in front of the ruins. Check out the size of those snouts."

He did and was duly impressed. "Don't want to tangle with those creatures. I'll stick with terrorists. No snouts. Fewer teeth." He waited for a muddy pickup truck to pass and then pulled back onto the road.

His leg began to throb. "If it's much farther, I'll need to stop and stretch," he said.

"About five minutes more," Josette said, "but you can stop anytime you need to. I can drive and give you a break."

"I can handle five minutes."

"You don't have to, but if you do, take the next blacktop road to the right. There's no sign. People just call it Guillory Road. Dad's house is the only one on it."

Keenan took the road slowly, dodging as many of the bumps and muddy potholes as he could. The BMW had probably never experienced a ride as rough as this and never gotten half this dirty.

He'd find a way to get a first-class carwash before Bart had to face the mess.

The blacktop dead-ended at what appeared to serve as a graveled parking area. He spotted the tall outriggers on the shrimp boat before he saw the house.

The boat was anchored in a wide inlet of water that branched out from the even wider bayou. Apparently, the area had been drudged out to accommodate the large boat.

Finally, Keenan saw the roofline above a thick cluster of live oak trees with moss hanging from the lower branches. The house was built on stilts with a covered porch on the second level that faced the bayou.

The area beneath the house was relegated to storage, it seemed. He noticed ice coolers, buckets and various tools. An SUV that looked to be about five or more years old was parked beneath the back cover of the steps.

The paint on the house was peeling and the fading shutters were askew. But there was a woman's touch, too. A rocking chair and several plaid, cotton porch-swing pillows made the area look almost homey.

"Dad's pickup truck isn't here," Josette said. "So much for his waiting until we could talk before he made any quick decisions."

"Did he promise that?"

"No. He came closer to saying that I wasn't wanted or needed in any decision-making. You're likely thinking I got what I deserve, then."

"Not thinking that at all. I'd know something was seriously off-kilter in my dad's thinking if he suddenly decided to stop raising his prize beef cattle."

"You mentioned that your grandfather had a small ranch north of Nashville. I didn't realize your father was also a rancher."

"My parents do it for a living. For Grandpa, it is his life. That and keeping Grandma happy."

"Sounds like a beautiful family," she said almost wistfully. "Stable." He was sure she was comparing it to her own and finding the Guillorys lacking.

"Who drives the SUV?" Keenan asked, eager to change the subject.

"It belongs to Lorraine Cormier, but her son, Daniel, drives it as often as she does."

"What's Lorraine's story?"

"She's Dad's on-again, off-again 'girlfriend,'" Josette said. "I'm not sure which at any given time. Not that it matters. I don't think Dad always knows, either."

"Does she live nearby?"

"A few miles down the road. She owns the popular Cormier Shrimp and Crab Shack restaurant and rents out several cabins along the bayou."

"Do people really vacation out here with these terrifying bayou creatures?" The long snout and big teeth of the alligator he'd seen a few moments ago still had him freaked out.

"More than you'd think. Lorraine has had paying guests from as far away as Australia. Louisiana bayous are world-famous, though admittedly most renters come from the small towns up and down the bayou. If they start having themselves too good a time at the Crab Shack after a night of partying, she convinces them to rent one of her fishing cabins. No drunk driving allowed."

Keenan observed everything around him, a routine reaction when he entered a new environment. He'd been in enough dangerous situations as an FBI agent that he never took safety for granted.

"Seems like it could get lonesome out here sometimes," Keenan said.

"It can get lonesome anywhere if the right person isn't with you," Josette said.

"How true," Keenan agreed. Admittedly, he'd been too busy with his career to notice, but during this medical leave, the loneliness had crept in. He wondered what Josette's life was like in Nashville. Sure, she was an in-demand designer, but from the sound of it, she had room for someone in her life. Too bad it couldn't be him.

"At least Lorraine has her son, Daniel, to keep her company," Josette said.

"How old is Daniel?" Keenan asked.

"Twenty. Two years younger than I am. He and I were close friends when we were growing up. Many an afternoon when I was staying with Dad the two of us grabbed a pirogue for a few hours of exploring."

"Just a friendship?"

"Definitely. Once we reached our teens and I was here visiting my father, the exploring gave way to music, books, movies, and boys back in New York for me and to shrimping for him."

When it was clear Antoine wasn't there but dodging them somewhere, they entered the house. Keenan figured the desolate location allowed her father to keep his door unlocked. They went into the kitchen and made a fresh pot of coffee. It was almost a half hour later and they were thinking of heading back into New Orleans before they heard a vehicle pull up in front of the house.

Josette checked it out and Keenan followed her, noticing a beat-up panel truck with "Cormier Shrimp and Crab Shack" written along the side in a peeling wrap.

"Lorraine has arrived," Josette told him. "She'll let herself in, never thinks of herself as a guest, just as an almost live-in. I'm sure she'll have plenty to say about Antoine giving up on shrimping and a comfortable income, not that I've ever heard Antoine mention marriage. Don't know if he'll ever divorce my mom."

Lorraine joined them in the kitchen. The two women exchanged cool hellos but offered no introductions.

"Do you know where Dad is this morning?" Josette asked.

"He had to make an emergency delivery to a restaurant in Houma. At least that's where he said he was going. Who knows these days?" Keenan didn't need extensive training to pick up Lorraine's attitude. The woman was none too pleased with Antoine. Or Josette, for that matter. She hadn't even more than glanced his way, either.

"I talked to him last night and told him we'd be here early this morning," Josette said. "I guess the shrimp order was more important."

Keenan sized Lorraine up as best he could without being obvious. He wasn't really interested in her physical appearance but making preliminary judgments about what you'd be dealing with was part and parcel of being in law enforcement.

Unless, of course, the woman looked like Josette. Lorraine didn't. She wore faded jeans, a size or two too small, had shoulder-length dark hair pulled into a ponytail. No makeup. Keenan guessed her age to be in the midforties.

"We can only wait an hour at most to see Dad," Josette said. "We have to be back in town for an important appointment."

Lorraine shrugged, proving she didn't care about their itinerary. "I thought Antoine was your important appointment," she tossed over her shoulder as she walked over to the pantry and pulled a huge pot from a bottom shelf.

Josette followed her. "You must be as upset about Dad's threat to sell the shrimp boat as I am."

Lorraine set the pot on the counter. "Why would I be? He can sell it if he wants. Buy a dozen more. Buy two or three dozen more. He's married to a multimillionaire."

Keenan had wondered when wealth was going to come up. Unless there was a prenuptial agreement that didn't affect anything at this point anyway, Antoine Guillory should have adequate income for anything he wanted and that included a new shrimp boat and a new wife.

Lorraine turned to him and swept her sharp black eyes over him, as if assessing him and finding him unworthy. "I hope you're not another of Josette's worthless detectives," she said with disdain.

She turned back to Josette. "If he is, keep him away from Antoine. Your dad's sick and tired of Detective Hyde hanging around, hounding him with questions about Isadora's disappearance a year after the fact."

"I won't argue the worthless part with you," Keenan said, "but I'm not a detective. I just came along for the ride." Keenan stuck out his hand. "Keenan Carter. Nice to meet you."

She ignored his hand and looked at him suspiciously. "Are you a cop? You look like one."

"Not a cop," Keenan answered. "Just here to check out the bayou scene."

"We're both in New Orleans for a friend's wedding," Josette explained. "Keenan was nice enough to volunteer to fight the traffic for me this morning."

Lorraine rubbed the back of her neck, her facial muscles appearing strained. "I'm on a tight schedule myself today, getting ready for Fat Tuesday."

"Big celebration?" Keenan asked.

"Yes, and growing bigger every year," she answered, the first note of civility slipping into her voice. "We have a huge crawfish Mardi Gras celebration at our family restaurant. Full house. Zydeco and dancing into the night. All the cabins are rented."

"Sounds like fun," Keenan said truthfully. "I haven't been to a crawfish boil since I graduated LSU."

"If you're still in New Orleans, you two should come by. I'll take all the profit I can get," Lorraine said.

With an invitation like that, Keenan figured, how could they resist?

"I just might do that," Josette said.

I, not *we,* he noticed, obviously not including him.

Lorraine grabbed the pot and hefted it in her arms. "If you see Antoine, tell him I took this."

"Will do."

"Interesting woman," Keenan said, as he closed the door behind Lorraine.

"She can be. I've never seen her quite like that," Josette admitted.

"Who's Detective Hyde?"

"Max Hyde. He's the New Orleans detective who's in charge of Mother's missing person case. That's the first I've heard of his harassing Dad. I need to find out what's going on with that."

Keenan would like to know, too. What reason would Detective Hyde have for continually questioning the estranged husband of the missing woman?

Unless he suspected Antoine Guillory knew something he wasn't telling.

Chapter Six

Josette expected at least a decent welcome from her father. All she got when he showed up was a dismissive hug and a failed attempt at a smile.

"I thought we agreed it wasn't necessary for you to make a trip down here today," Antoine said.

"I know it isn't necessary," Josette admitted, "but I discovered I had the morning free, and I really wanted to see you."

Antoine nodded out the door. "Good-looking vehicle out there. Doesn't look like a rental to me."

"No," Josette answered. "The car belongs to Addison's husband-to-be. He was nice enough to loan it to us."

"Us?"

Keenan stepped out of the bathroom and joined them in the small living area. Josette introduced him as a friend who was also in town for the wedding.

"Keenan Carter," Antoine repeated. "Any chance you're the same Keenan Carter who quarterbacked LSU to a national championship a few years back?"

"That's me."

"You were one of the best. Too bad you got injured before you made it to the NFL."

"That was crushing at the time," Keenan admitted, "but I moved past it. No cheering fans and big paychecks, but on the bright side, I don't wake up bruised and sore every Monday morning."

"You still got a limp there, I see. What are you doing to get that?"

"Nothing at the moment."

Josette was thankful Keenan hadn't mentioned the FBI. Antoine was still complaining endlessly about the way law enforcement handled Isadora's investigation last Mardi Gras. No use in making an immediate bad impression with him.

"Was Lorraine still here when you arrived?" Antoine asked.

"She arrived a few minutes after us. We talked for a few minutes before she rushed back to the restaurant. With your pot."

He took off his cap and ran his hand through his thick, wavy dark hair. "Guess she threw in her two cents' worth on whether or not I should sell my boat."

"Let's just say her opinions were not as I expected."

"Don't let that bother you. They change by the minute."

"None of us fully understands, Dad. Of course, it's your money and you can spend it any way you like, but why the sudden urge to give up your livelihood?"

"Why are you suddenly so worried about how I live my life, Josette? I've already sold the *Lady Isadora*. The money will transfer hands by Tuesday."

He tossed the cap onto the scarred coffee table and turned. "Now I need some fresh coffee and to get this fishy smell off me."

Antoine walked toward the back of the house and she and Keenan went into the kitchen and started another pot of coffee. Coffee was fast becoming their solution for everything. Too bad it had never answered even one of their questions. But then, what had?

"Dad seems dead set on selling the shrimp boat," Josette said when her father went into the bathroom.

"It appears he's already sold it. He could have a good reason for his decision," Keenan said.

"Hit me with a few of them."

"Maybe health concerns that he hasn't wanted to tell you about."

"He assured me last night that his health was fine. Of course, I guess he could just be trying to protect me from worrying."

"He could just feel the need to move on, try on a new lifestyle," Keenan offered.

"Not Dad. This is his life. He needed it more than he needed the woman he loved. That's why he refused to even consider moving to New York."

"People change," Keenan said. "He may be reconsidering life with Isadora. Sometimes life forces a person to change. I've read that large seafood importing companies are taking a much bigger share of the profits than they did a few years back. He may no longer think the financial benefits are worth the work."

"Legally, half of Mother's wealth is his. But he's never touched it. Claims it isn't his and he doesn't need it. He makes enough to get by with his shrimp-ing business."

"Perhaps you'd have a better chance of getting Antoine to open up if I'm not around," Keenan sug-gested. "I'll go outside and check out the fancy shrimp boat. Who knows? Maybe I'll buy it."

"For netting terrorists? But leaving me alone with Dad is probably a good idea."

"Can't hurt. Call me when you get ready to go and I'll meet you at the car."

"Be careful," Josette warned. "If you go for a walk and follow the inlet, you'll eventually reach a boggy area that you could seriously get lost in."

"I promise to stay clear of bogs and away from snakes and alligators," he said. "Good luck with An-toine but remember, it's his life. You can't protect him from it any more than you can make decisions for your mother."

He took her hand and gave it a squeeze before he started toward the door. She knew he intended it to be a comforting gesture, a reassuring one, so why did her breath catch and smoky desire curl inside her? There was no explaining her every reaction to his touch, so this time she didn't try.

KEENAN WALKED OVER to the *Lady Isadora* and jumped aboard. It smelled of shrimp, dead fish and the damp, musky odors of the bayou even though the deck had obviously been scrubbed down. The nets were clean and appeared ready for use.

Winches, ropes, cables and such made the deck

difficult to maneuver. The culling table was as large as his grandfather's old family dining table, easily spacious enough to hold a full net of shrimp and several pounds of unwanted sea life to be thrown out to the gulls.

He glanced into the galley. It was spotless, smelled like cleanser and easily big enough for the basic requirements of a kitchen. There was a sink, cooktop, table, four folding chairs and a dorm-sized refrigerator.

The ice to keep the day's catch cold was no doubt loaded into the hold, as needed. A small TV was bracketed above the sink. He wasn't sure if that was for entertainment, keeping up with the weather or both. There was also a radio and mic setup, no doubt for relaying info to other boaters or requesting help.

The wheelhouse looked comfortable. The lumpy bunks in the two-bedroom cabin not so much. Three pairs of rubber boots sat near the back of the deck.

Keenan wondered what a boat in mint condition as this one would sell for. Probably enough to support the apparently simple lifestyle of Antoine Guillory for quite a while.

But Josette was right. To sell it meant not only to lose this lifestyle but to give up the livelihood he'd depended on all his life. So why now?

It couldn't be because he couldn't bear life without Isadora. According to Josette, he hadn't shared a home with her in years. Not to mention, he'd gone without seeing her for long periods of time, especially when she pulled her disappearing acts.

Whatever the reason for selling the boat, Antoine clearly did not want Josette involved.

As an agent, Keenan was generally suspicious of people's motives. Even more so when they acted out of character. He thought about Detective Max Hyde. Why was he still pressing Antoine for answers? Had he discovered evidence to suggest there was foul play involved in Isadora's disappearance?

Was Antoine involved? If so, that might explain why he was ready to clear out of the area. Was Antoine trying to keep Josette out of this to protect her from something or someone?

That possibility was cause enough for Keenan to stick around even without official power or authority. Nothing stopped him from operating as a friend.

A friend, or had he moved past that a heartbeat or two ago?

JOSETTE HAD ALWAYS felt at home at Antoine's house. Today, as she waited for her father to shower, she felt like a stranger. Worse, she felt unwanted, as if she were snooping, digging into his private life.

It was exactly what she was doing and yet she continued, working quickly, not knowing what she hoped to find.

At first sight, everything looked familiar. One basket of clean work clothes in the laundry room, two baskets of clothes ready for the wash with a large bottle of liquid detergent waiting next to them.

There was also a large cloth hamper of dirty linens, napkins and greasy aprons from Lorraine's restaurant.

Lorraine frequently used his extra-large washing machine for big loads, especially when her cabins were all rented. Nothing unusual.

She stepped into his bedroom next. What she found there stopped her in her tracks. A small travel bag held his shaving equipment and various toiletries, all packed and ready to stow inside his larger suitcase that lay open on the bed.

She picked up a large envelope beside the luggage. Nothing inside. No plane tickets. No passport, but those could always be added at the last minute.

She unzipped a faded blue duffel bag up by the pillows. Clean, folded casual clothes, none realistically suitable for working the shrimp boats all day.

Her father was getting ready to travel? Where?

She could hear cups and spoons clatter in the kitchen. She hurried to rezip the duffel but she thought she saw something shiny inside. A flash of something.

She started to unzip the bag and take a second look.

"Josette?"

At the sound of her father's voice, she spun around, expecting to see him in the doorway, a demanding look on his stern face as he asked why she was rummaging in his private gear. Luckily, he was calling her from the kitchen. She left the bag and joined him there. She sat across from him at a scratched wooden table that he'd had all her life.

"Did we lose Keenan?" Antoine asked as he gestured to the coffee he'd poured for them.

"He went outside to check out the bayou scene and give us a little privacy."

"Thoughtful. How'd he get that limp?"

"He says it's a work-related injury."

"Exactly what kind of work would that be?"

She considered pretending not to know. But she'd never flat out lied to her father, and she really didn't want to start now. Lies had a way of tangling you in their web.

"Keenan's an FBI agent in the counterterrorism division," she admitted.

"When were you planning to tell me that?"

"I wasn't because that has nothing to do with us. He's on medical leave until he completes his rehab. He's in New Orleans only as Bart Gordon's best man."

Antoine looked skeptical. "You claim you just met him, and yet he's here with you today."

"He has no ulterior motive in being here if that's what you're suggesting. He's not here on FBI business concerning Mother's disappearance."

"Good." Antoine nodded his agreement. "Let's keep it that why. Max Hyde does enough of that."

"I don't see how Max can justify spending so much time in this area," Josette said. "It's not as if he's making any progress with finding Mother."

"Word on the bayou is that Max is working a murder case involving one of the cartels. Doesn't take much for some fool to end up owing them more than he can pay, and they have their own way to collect their debts."

Josette grimaced. "I didn't realize the cartels had become such a problem here."

"They're a problem everywhere they can get a foot inside the door, especially when they're working from a major city like New Orleans."

"Is that why you're selling out?"

He picked up his coffee mug and swallowed a mouthful. "No. You don't need to worry about me, Boo. I know my way around the shrimping business."

Using one of his favorite nicknames for Josette didn't totally reassure her this time.

Lorraine had likely called it right.

This had to do with Isadora.

Josette began nailing her father with questions the way the paparazzi had Friday night.

"Have you heard from Mother?

"Have you heard something about her from someone else?

"Do you believe the rumor that she's planning to reappear on Mardi Gras?

"Is she coming back to her show?"

Antoine didn't respond to any of them, which was all the answer she needed. "She's my mother. I have a right to know whatever you know."

He rested his elbows on the table and massaged his temples. "I suppose you do, but you have to promise me one thing. You can tell no one what I'm about to tell you. No one, especially not Mr. FBI."

Her body stiffened. She had no idea where this was going, but it couldn't be good.

KEENAN FOUND A pair of boots large enough to fit over his shoes. He only had one pair of sneakers with him and he didn't want them to get wet and muddy on his first full day in Louisiana.

He stepped off the boat. Two large turtles sunning on a log jumped into the water, reminding him of the alligators who'd slid into the bayou earlier. He went back to the car for his trusty Smith and Wesson and his waistband holster. He wasn't going alligator hunting, but just in case one decided to attack, he'd be ready.

He began the trek along the bank of the narrow inlet. A sleek, shiny crappie dangled from the beak of a regal gray heron that had just caught its breakfast. He spotted two river otters playing in the water near the opposite bank.

A yellow wasp dived at him and hungry mosquitoes buzzed at his ears. He slapped them away.

After a few yards, he stopped walking and checked his surroundings. The area was still calm and peaceful except for an occasional splash from a fish and the loud cawing of a murder of crows fussing at him from the needle-loaded branches of a cluster of cypress trees. He stepped around the knotty cypress knees that stretched into the water.

A hand-sized black spider fell from a tree and landed on his shirtsleeve. He knocked it away quickly, almost tripping on a tangle of vines.

A few more yards and boggy water began to flood the low-lying lands. Fronds of huge palmetto plants intermingled with thick brush and stubbly cottonwood trees. Trunks of fallen trees lay haphazardly amongst the brush.

It was as if he'd reached the other world Josette had

mentioned and he began to understand why people fell in love with life along a bayou.

Just as he turned to follow the inlet back toward the shrimp boat, he caught a glimpse of movement in the peripheral of his vision. For a second, he could have sworn it was human, but when he looked again all he saw was a flock of egrets on the move.

He continued on and when he had the shrimp boat in his view, he heard the unmistakable sounds of gunfire behind him in the distance.

Drawing his weapon, he turned and crouched low behind a palmetto frond. His eyes scanned the dense foliage and— There! He caught movement. This time it was no flock of birds. A person was running helter-skelter toward the bayou, a gun held chest high as he or she fired.

Warning shots…or was the gunman firing at someone Keenan couldn't see?

His instincts kicked into overdrive and he took cover. Fearful that Josette or Antoine would exit the house and be hit by an errant bullet, he started toward the figure. The pain in his left thigh flared hot as he scrambled along the uneven, boggy terrain. He struggled to keep the gunman in his view as his vision was blocked by low-hanging vines. Nevertheless, he charged ahead, gaining on the figure, when his dragging left foot hit the root of a cypress tree and he plunged headfirst into the dirt.

Pain speared him and he grasped his leg. But he couldn't stop. He had to know what the gunman was doing near the Guillory place and he couldn't let Josette venture into the line of fire. Forcing himself to stand, he dragged in a ragged breath and trudged on.

But the gunman was nowhere in sight.

He spun in every direction for a few minutes. *Too long*, he thought. He had made himself a target if the gunman was still in firing distance.

Angry and disappointed, he turned toward Antoine's house just as his phone dinged. A text from Josette.

Ready to go. NOW.

By the time he reached the house, she was already in the car. There was no sign of Antoine.

He had an idea the ride home would not be pleasant.

Especially when he told her what he'd met in the bayou.

Chapter Seven

The watcher's hands were sweaty, breath quick and painful. One pull on the trigger and Josette's blood would pool in Antoine Guillory's driveway.

Her death might pass as accidental, a reckless firing of a weapon from someone shooting indiscriminately out in the bayou or from the swampy bog behind her dad's house.

Only once the body was identified, the accidental aspect wouldn't fly. The investigation into Isadora's daughter's death would be all-consuming.

Better to hold off and stick with the original plan. There was no reason for it not to work unless Josette started nosing around and ruined everything. Antoine wouldn't let that happen as long as he remained convinced that his ex-wife was not only alive but needed him.

The watcher could trust Antoine, but what about the stranger? Was he Josette's lover? Her bodyguard? Possibly a new detective. Maybe someone who already knew too much.

Better to get the business over with and get out of

this area fast. Time was running out. Either the plan came together quickly or there would be no choice but to kill or be killed. The watcher hated to kill. But if it came down to live or die, there would be no contest.

Chapter Eight

Josette watched the house's roofline and the tall outriggers of the shrimp boat shrink and finally disappear from the side-view mirror. Her nerves were a
ragged mess.

If only she could believe that her dad had received
the truth. But there was no hard evidence that Isadora
had indeed communicated with a friend that she was
alive and well.

Antoine claimed he didn't know Isadora's exact
location, nor would he share the identity of the so-
called friend.

All Antoine admitted was that Isadora was alive
and well and would be returning on her own time.

None of which explained Antoine's sudden rush
to sell the *Lady Isadora* nor to turn away from the
only life he'd ever known.

And it certainly didn't explain why he had packed
luggage on his bed. If Isadora was returning, why
was Antoine leaving? And where did he plan to go?

Josette rubbed her temples as the questions ping-
ponged in her mind. About the only thing she knew

for certain was that her father was acting totally out of character and she had no reasonable explanation for it. Apparently, neither did Detective Max Hyde.

For the first time, she wondered if Antoine was connected to her mother's disappearance.

"Are you okay?" Keenan said after several minutes of silence. "You seem upset, depressed."

She forced a smile she didn't feel. "I'll work on that," she said. "Can't be a party pooper at all the wedding events."

"You can never be a party pooper. Addison won't allow it. But talking about whatever your dad said that has made you even more uncomfortable than you were before might help."

She'd love to tell Keenan the full truth and get his take on everything. But she took her promise to her dad seriously.

"There's not much new to say other than that Dad really is selling the boat and it has nothing to do with Isadora."

"And you're not quite buying that?"

"I'd love to, but when I think about it, everything in his life has always centered around Mom. Right or wrong, they share a bond that I'll never understand. The whole situation has me totally frustrated."

"Then we should probably change the subject. I won't ask more, but if selling the boat is prompted by a sudden need for cash, I'd encourage you to go to the police or the FBI. And the sooner, the better."

"Not you, too. Dad is not one who'd ever get involved in something illegal." She said the words but couldn't stop the niggling doubt that prevented her from totally believing them. She knew her father was not telling her everything. She just didn't know why. Was he in over his head? Had he—

She stopped the thought before it formed. What was she thinking? This was her father. The man who loved her and her mother. She knew him, and knew he'd never do anything to harm either of them.

Again, she wished she could lay everything out on the table and get Keenan's professional opinion. But she couldn't. And it hurt her to hold back the truth from him.

Keenan broke into her thoughts. "I'm not accusing him of anything. I'm just saying that danger can sometimes find innocent victims."

"I appreciate all your help, Keenan. I really do, but I'm starting to feel really bad about dragging you into this when you should be hanging out with your old LSU buddies and partaking in the carnival spirit— or spirits."

"Forget my buddies. You're cuter by far. And you know I can't resist a mystery." He hesitated a moment, then added, "Speaking of mysteries…"

She turned to look at him and tucked her hair behind her ears. "Another one? I don't know if I can take it."

"Sorry, Josette, but there's something I have to tell you. Back there, when I went down by the shrimp boat, I took a walk along the bayou. I heard gunshots and I saw a gunman. I followed him—or her—but

I tripped." He let out a curse. "When I got up, they were gone."

She looked at him, trying to assess him. "Why would you follow anyone with a gun?"

"I'm in law enforcement, Josette. I don't run from trouble. Especially when you're involved." He shot her a glance and she saw the worry in his eyes. "I was afraid whoever it was would be shooting when you came outside."

The same fear she saw in his expression, she felt in her chest. What if Keenan had been shot? It seemed they'd known each other for the blink of an eye, but she'd already come to care about him. A bullet ripping through him was not an image she wished to envision.

"Did you get a look at the shooter?" she asked him, eager to solve *this* mystery, at least.

He shook his head. "I couldn't even tell if it was a male or female. Not through the foliage. All I know is whoever it was wore dark pants and a dark long-sleeve shirt."

"I'll need to tell my father. Warn him to be careful," she said.

"There's someone else we should tell," he replied.

Josette knew immediately he meant Detective Max Hyde.

"When was the last time you talked to Mr. Personality?"

"Five or six months ago. During the first few weeks after Mother went missing, Max called me every day, but the story never changed. No sign of foul play, though they couldn't completely rule it out.

No new leads in the investigation. No credible sightings they hadn't checked out."

"Yeah. Gets that way when the leads start to dry up, especially in a situation like this where the previous success rate is zero. Would you mind if I talk to the detective, not as an FBI agent but as your concerned friend?"

"Now that you mention it, I should probably at least try to talk to him myself while I'm here. But there's no use for you to get stuck with that task. I can't imagine when you'd find the time, Mr. Best Man."

"*My* finding time is not the issue. With Mardi Gras in full swing, every available police officer in town is likely pulling extra shifts. The earliest Hyde would be able to fit us in is probably Thursday or Friday after Ash Wednesday, if then."

"Don't you have a flight out after the wedding?"

"Yes, Tuesday morning, but I can change it. It's not like I'm rushing back to a job."

She hesitated, then asked the question she wanted an answer to. "You must have someone expecting you back in Nashville."

He shook his head. "I won't be going back to Nashville. I only caught the plane there because I'd been visiting my grandparents. I live in DC. And no one is waiting for me there. What about you? Someone waiting for you in Nashville?"

"No. I'm a loner workaholic."

"Then you don't mind if I give the detective a call," he asked.

"I can't ask you to get that involved in my problems," she insisted.

"Trying to get rid of me again?"

"I'm trying *not* to take advantage of you."

"I'm volunteering."

"In that case, I should warn you that I could get used to all this teaming up with you." She didn't know how she managed to hide the smile that threatened to appear.

"Still getting no argument from me. I'll try to get in touch with Detective Hyde while you drink tea this afternoon."

ANTOINE GUILLORY STOOD on the porch long after Josette and Keenan had driven out of sight. His daughter had sworn to keep everything he'd told her a secret, but what if he hadn't told her everything? And what if what he'd told her was all a lie?

What if Isadora wasn't alive?

What if the ache that was shredding his heart like shards of glass could never go away? How could he go on living without Isadora?

But Antoine had no choice but to believe what he'd told her was true. He had nothing left to live on but hope.

He would have to depend on that for now.

JOSETTE SIPPED FROM her flowered china cup and savored the taste of the lemongrass herbal tea. Switching from angst to relaxation in such short time hadn't been easy, but the laughter and breezy conversation flowing around her facilitated the mood shift.

The surroundings didn't hurt, either. The tearoom was plush and beautifully decorated, totally capturing the old-world feeling. The refreshments had been served with just the correct touch of British flair.

Someone tinkled the keys on a grand piano, softly enough that guests didn't have to yell to be heard over the music.

Josette decided this was the perfect way to calm her nerves and soothe her soul leading up to the big event, especially with the wildness of Mardi Gras having taken over the city. The best part was that after they'd gone through introductions and/or greetings with a dozen or so other guests, she, Addison and the two bridesmaids had been ushered to a table for four.

Sara, Beth, Addison and Josette had been practically inseparable during their four years at LSU. They'd shared everything except boyfriends and underwear. Even best friends had to draw the line somewhere.

Sara looked and acted much the same. Short, shapely, blonde and bubbly. And super fun.

Beth was tall, willowy, with lustrous brown curls that cascaded past her shoulders. She could have been a model if she hadn't fallen madly in love with a much older med student during her sophomore year.

Beth reached to the crystal tiered tray in the center of their table and chose one of the petite tea sandwiches. "You guys can sip your tea and ignore the food as long as you like. I'm starved."

"I'm still deciding which one to try first," Sara said. "They all look delicious."

Beth took a bite of her cucumber and cream cheese treat. "Isn't anyone going to ask me why I'm starving?"

"All you've had to eat today is airplane food?" Addison guessed.

"Nope."

"You're on a weird diet," Sara said, "like that cabbage concoction you choked down every morning for weeks during our freshman year?"

"You *would* bring that up. Makes me nauseous to think about it, but then everything makes me nauseous these days."

"Nauseous… Oh, my God! Are you pregnant?" Addison squealed.

Beth pushed back from the table, stood and patted a barely discernable baby bump.

Everyone jumped up and dove into a round of squeals and hugs.

"How far along are you?" Josette asked.

"Three months, I've been to the OB and it's for real."

"I can't believe you've kept this a secret," Sara said.

Beth beamed. "I wanted to tell you all at once and in person. I don't mean to steal any of your thunder, Addison, but I couldn't hold it in another second."

"Don't even think about that," Addison said. "It just adds a new kind of magic to the celebration."

"Is there any problem with the bridesmaid dress fitting?" Josette asked. "If there is, I have a needle and thread with me at all times. I can let out a seam in minutes."

"The dress fits fine, but I did worry at first that I might outgrow your gorgeous design before I got to wear it."

Sara shook her head and her short blond curls danced about her rosy cheeks. "I'm in a state of mild shock. I never expected you to be the first of the four of us to get pregnant."

"Why not? I was the first to get married."

"Yes, but what happened to all that talk of not getting tied down with children until you were thirty?"

"Everyone has the right to change their mind. Besides, John is thirty-two and after the demands of his residencies, he can't wait to start a family."

"Then he must be thrilled."

"Over the top. He's spoiling me rotten."

"He has always spoiled you rotten," Addison quipped.

"One of his best qualities," Beth teased.

"Guess we're growing up," Sara said. "Who'd have ever thought it would happen so fast?"

"It's not all that fast," Beth said. "I'll be twenty-four next week."

Josette would be twenty-three by the end of summer, but she wasn't ready to think of marriage or babies. Her mother always managed to drain much of Josette's emotional strength. Getting her career up and running took what was left of that and all of her energy.

She hadn't even had a date since before her mother had gone missing.

"What's new with you, Sara?" Josette asked.

"I broke up with Doug. A friendly parting of the ways. Our lifestyles didn't mesh. On the bright side, I got a great promotion last month."

"Super and I'm sure well deserved," Josette said. "Will you have to move?"

"No, but I will have to do more traveling. That's one of the things I love most about the job. Next week I fly to London for a meeting. After that, I'm setting up a new software program in Finland."

"You always loved an adventure." Addison reached for a tea tidbit. "Your turn to spill the beans, Josette. I know your career's hot, but how's your love life?"

"On a scale of one to ten, I'd have to say zero," Josette said. "I'm so busy that if I took a lover, he'd have to make an appointment for us to have sex."

"Rumor has it, you went off on a romp this morning with Bart's best man who is said to be so hot, he has to wear a combustible warning," Sara said, waving her hand in front of her face like a fan.

"It wasn't a romp. More like a traffic jam to the bayou."

"Yes, but is he hot?" Beth pressed. "Again, scale of one to ten?"

"I'd say somewhere in the neighborhood of twenty."

"Really?"

"Just joking. He's a nice guy but I didn't do a heat index on him." Oh, who was she kidding? She'd assessed him in the airplane.

"I may have to try him out on the dance floor at the ball tonight," Sara said. "That is, unless you're staking a claim."

Josette held up her hands, palm out. "No claims, guaranteed."

Dancing at the ball. Josette hadn't even thought of that. She wasn't sure Keenan would dance at all with his bad leg apparently still giving him pain.

But he might ask her to dance to something slow and sultry that didn't require much of his wounded leg. She could see it now. Her head on his shoulder. The heat from his body sizzling through hers.

Her pulse raced and she forced herself to stop thinking such wildly titillating thoughts. She refused to go gaga over a man she'd just met, especially with all that was going on with her parents.

The talk switched to the dresses they were wearing tonight. It was decided they'd all four gather in the Princess Suite to fine-tune their makeup and coiffures just as they used to do before a party at LSU.

They munched between chatter and were still engrossed in the conversation when the waitress arrived with a tiered tray of decadent desserts.

Josette was just about to choose a calorie-laden sweet when Sara leaned in close.

"Don't look now, Josette, but there's a woman a few tables to the left who's been staring at you ever since she sat down. Her group is apparently not part of Addison's party."

Josette turned just enough to catch a glimpse of the attractive middle-aged lady. As soon as she locked eyes with her, the woman turned away. Josette didn't recognize her, but that wasn't surprising. Strangers frequently recognized Josette as Isadora's daughter.

Fans who'd watched Isadora play Jill Hawthorne for years tended to think of Isadora as a friend. They'd walk right up and tell her how much they loved her mother.

Always much worse, of course, when she was out with Isadora and subject to the paparazzi stalking. It had taken Josette a long time to realize that though her mother complained, she actually thrived on the adoration.

She cast another casual glance over her shoulder and noticed the lady looking her way again. This time the stranger's gaze remained constant and her brows knotted.

Who was she? And what did she want with Josette?

She turned her attention back to her friends. Right now she heard a lemon tart calling her name.

HOURS LATER, under the moonlight, the four friends climbed out of their chauffeured town car and were welcomed into the lavish lobby of a downtown hotel by an attendant in tails.

"One more quick selfie before we head to the ballroom," Addison said.

"Another one?" Sara groaned.

Addison patted loose locks of her gorgeous hair and pulled them all closer before snapping yet another photo. "I want every second of this weekend preserved in pictures."

Beth tugged on the back of her dress. "Are you sure this gown doesn't look too tight from the back?" she asked. "It fit perfectly last week."

"You look marvelous, as always," Josette said.

"I wish John could have come," Beth said. "One of your cousins at high tea said the band tonight is supposed to be great."

"Why didn't he come?" Addison asked.

"He's on call and he didn't want to screw up the rotation. That's one of the disadvantages to being married to a neurosurgeon. Their time is not always their own. Besides, he said I'd have a better time hanging out with you three."

"He's got a point," Addison said. "We've barely stopped talking since we got together and I'm just getting warmed up."

"On with the party," Sara said as she herded them together. "The invitation says eight o'clock, and it's already eight thirty."

"We have to be a little late if we want to make a grand entrance, just like the Fab Four of old," Josette said.

Sara laughed. "Which no one ever called us but ourselves."

Addison handed everyone their ticket. "Can't get in without this," she warned.

Addison's parents' reputation as philanthropists had landed them several invitations to various Mardi Gras balls. Her dad had decided on one of the most elite; a formal celebration famous for its great food, top-shelf booze, a popular band and lots of important guests.

They took the crowded escalator to the third-floor ballroom and forfeited their ticket stubs. They were greeted by waiters passing around cocktails and flutes of champagne. The band was playing a rocking version of, "They All Asked for You," a standard in New Orleans, especially during Mardi Gras.

A few people were second lining around the room. Most were clustered in small groups, talking and sipping their drink of choice.

Josette scanned the room for Keenan. He was standing with his buddies near one of the crowded bar areas. Her pulse raced and she found herself staring until he noticed and gave her a sexy wink. As terrific as he'd looked in a pair of jeans, the tux took top billing.

A craving like she'd never known burned inside her and, given half a chance, she knew she'd never stay out of his arms tonight.

"Josette. World to Josette, come in, please."

She spun around to Addison. "What? Did I miss something?"

"Nothing as important as drooling over Keenan while we're having an important conversation here."

"Don't let us stop you," Beth said. "You've got your priorities straight. Hunks before gossip."

"I wasn't drooling, was I?" She grinned at her friends then leaned in close. "Who are we gossiping about?" she whispered.

Addison spoke for the group. "The flaunting of a

magnitude of sparkling jewels by a roomful of New Orleans socialites."

"And my guess is all that glitters here is the real thing," Josette offered. "Likely not a cubic zirconia in the place."

"No shortage of shapely bodies to fill the slinky gowns and dangle the diamonds, either," Addison said. "I'll go and let Bart know we're here before he forgets he's off the market."

"Like you have a worry," Sara said. "That guy's so wrapped up in you, I doubt he even knows there are other women here."

Josette agreed, but there weren't just beautiful young women at the ball, there were females and males of all ages. All looked to be having a marvelous time except for one man she'd judge to be about the same age as her father. He looked as if he was being tortured as his wife kept pulling him back into the second-line dance.

That's how her parents would have looked at a festivity such as this. Isadora would have been the center of attention, dancing, twirling, flirting. Antoine would have been miserable, yearning to be home gulping down a cold beer while watching a game of anything that was played with a ball or getting ready for the next run for shrimp.

Despite that, she wished more than anything, they were both here tonight. Her missing mother, her mysterious father. What was going on with both of them?

Before she could ponder the question, another waiter in a white jacket stepped in front of them with a tray of decadent shrimp and bacon canapés. Josette took one and then accepted a cosmopolitan to wash it down. Tonight, she told herself, she'd put aside her nonstop concerns about her parents and just have fun.

Sara got a refill of champagne. Beth turned down the drink but took a second canapé and a glass of sparkling water with lime.

Addison's parents walked up and guided them to their reserved table for the evening. Minutes later, the guys joined them as well, and the night's events got started with announcements, acknowledgments and special welcomes to the krewe's more well-known guests.

The Landrys were singled out for the many charities they'd supported over the past year.

And then came the parade of waiters serving the sit-down dinner and the place grew quieter as everyone began devouring the gourmet meal.

THEY WERE ALMOST three hours into the ball and Keenan was continuously checking his watch. What could possibly be more fun than spending an evening being entertained by a better-than-average dance band and watching other men spin the woman who had him all hot and bothered around the dance floor.

Not Josette's fault, of course. It wasn't as if he'd asked her to dance or rather to endure his awkward attempts.

She was smooth and graceful, whether it was a belly-hugging ballad or a number that called for some fancy footwork. Her dress shimmered like tiny jewels. Her dark hair begged to have fingers tangle in it.

She was out of his league and he knew it.

The band played a few bars of the old Patsy Cline favorite, "Crazy." Couples began to fill the dance floor. Josette was standing several feet away from Keenan. She looked at him expectantly. He took a deep breath and decided to go for it. A second too late.

Moose walked up and asked her to dance.

He watched them for a moment and then before he could talk himself out of it, he maneuvered through the couples on the dance floor and tapped Moose on the shoulder.

Moose grinned and backed off. "All yours, sport. Don't waste it."

Josette stepped into Keenan's arms and put her lips to his ear. "I thought you were never going to ask."

Chapter Nine

Josette didn't take his hand but locked her fingers at the base of his neck, resting her head against his broad shoulder. She breathed in the woodsy, warm scent of him and felt the muscular strength in his arms as he pulled her even closer.

Her whole body tingled from a heated rush that left her dizzy with desire.

"I would have asked sooner," Keenan said, "but with this bum leg, I know I can't keep up with those moves you have."

"You're doing pretty good," she teased, hoping the shaking inside her wouldn't affect her voice. "You haven't stepped on my feet yet."

"Give me time. I have to say that you look devastatingly sexy in that dress. It shimmers like liquid gold."

She looked up at him and smiled. "Thank you. That was the intent."

"Is it one of your personal designs?"

"It is."

"Show it on the catwalk and you'd sell a million."

"I'd be satisfied with a half million to start." Her

eyes swept him from head to toe. "You do a lot for that tux yourself, lawman."

"Thanks. I feel like a stuffed peacock, especially with the Mardi Gras–colored bow tie and cummerbund."

"You have to be used to purple and gold if you played football at LSU."

"I was never a bow tie man."

His arms tightened around her and she lay her head back on his shoulder as the torch singer exaggerated every sultry note. Josette quit talking or thinking and melted into the desire that encompassed her. The song ended long before she was ready.

Another ballad started and she stayed in his arms. This time they barely moved, but just swayed together, holding on to each other, so close the hunger inside her grew dangerously unbridled.

The band took their break after that song. She and Keenan were the last to leave the floor.

It was just a dance, she reminded herself. They were strangers in the night, caught up in a magical infatuation that was too new to trust, though too hot to ignore.

They were only in New Orleans for a few more days.

As they were walking to their table, his hand resting on the small of her back, Josette had a hard time fighting the pull that drew her to Keenan. She wanted to throw caution to the wind and—

There was that woman again. The one she'd seen staring at her at high tea that afternoon. She was staring again, so intensely Josette felt as if she was looking right through her.

When Josette didn't look away, the woman started toward her. She was elegant, dripping diamonds, about the age of Isadora but not nearly as stunning. No one ever was.

Keenan dropped his hand and Josette stepped away from the table where the others in her party were sitting, just in case the conversation turned confrontational.

"I hope you don't mind my interrupting you," the woman said. "My name is Celeste Rubenstein."

The name didn't sound familiar to Josette. "Have we met?"

"No, but I saw you at high tea this afternoon. I wanted to come over and speak then but I needed something stronger than tea to give me courage to approach you."

Josette said nothing in return. She waited for Celeste to make her point.

"I suppose you know that you look exactly like Isadora Guillory. Everyone is talking about it."

"I'm her daughter."

"I thought so. You see, I met Isadora at this very ball last year and I'm still having trouble believing she hasn't been seen since."

Barely stopping for breath, Celeste took out her phone and pulled up a photo. "This is a picture my husband took of your mother and me at last year's ball. I treasure it." She handed over her phone for Josette to get a better look.

Josette's breath caught. It was her mother, wearing a shimmery, silk sapphire gown Josette had designed for her.

That in itself was shocking. As far as Josette knew, that was the first time Isadora had ever worn one of Josette's creations to a fancy event, though she'd designed several especially for her mother.

Isadora would always brag on Josette's creations and then hang them at the back of one of her gigantic closets never to be seen again. Whenever she went formal, Isadora would always choose from one of the famous and grossly expensive designers that red carpets seemed to love.

Isadora was smiling in the photo, her expressive eyes shining, her arm linked with Celeste's as if they were old friends. Her mother had likely taken such photos with countless men and women that night.

Suddenly, she registered what Celeste had said and goosebumps rose on her skin. "My mother attended this same ball last year, you said?"

"Yes." The woman shook her head in a sad, dejected gesture. "It was the last time she was seen in public."

"Do you have other pictures of Isadora?" Josette asked. She tried not to appear too pushy, but she was eager to see more photos. If this was her mom's last outing, perhaps Josette could get some clue what happened to her from the pictures.

"Yes, quite a few. She didn't show up until late, but she stayed until the band played the last number. Everyone was entranced by her."

Celeste took her phone and brought up another photo. "This is one of my favorites. She was second lining like a native and she got everyone up and dancing with her." She stepped closer to Josette, holding the phone between them so they both could see it.

Josette looked past her dancing and laughing mother, so full of life, to the static, shadowed figure some fifteen feet behind her. The man was partially hidden by other dancers and billowing purple and gold banners, but she could swear he looked familiar. She peered closer and pointed to the image. "Is that—"

Celeste brought the phone within inches of her eyes. "Yes, I do believe that's her costar Grant Gaines behind her. He must be going crazy without her."

Not likely. He'd certainly not overly cooperated with the detectives Josette had hired early into the investigation.

Her mother had constantly complained about having to spend so much time with him during the show's filming, but no matter how much she and Grant argued on the set, they were always all smiles in public and in the gossip mags.

The fans loved it that way.

But it was clear in this photo that he wasn't aware someone was capturing him on film. His hooded eyes were fixed on Isadora and the look he shot at her was far from adoration. She was reminded of the phrase, "If looks could kill…"

"I'm sorry, I don't have more pictures in my phone, but there are dozens of close-ups and group pictures featuring your mother on the disc the professional photographer put together. All the krewe members got a copy."

"How would I get my hands on one of those?"

"I can have a copy made of mine if you'd like. Tell me where you're staying and I can drop it by your hotel tomorrow afternoon if that's convenient for you."

"I'd love that. If I'm not there you can leave it at the front desk, and I'll pick it up. My name is Josette Guillory."

"Yes, I know."

Judging from the pictures, Isadora hadn't had a care the night before she'd disappeared. But what was driving her to stay away so long without a word to Josette or Antoine? It hurt to think that their fears and concerns meant that little to Isadora.

It was a lot more terrifying to consider worse possibilities.

Josette woke on Sunday morning to a light tapping at the door that separated her room from the rest of the Princess Suite. She checked her phone for the time. Ten after seven. That was a shocker. Addison had always been the one who had to be dragged out of bed after a late night.

"Come in," Josette called.

Addison pushed her way through the door, wearing the plush hotel robe and carrying two cups of coffee. "I was hoping you were awake."

"I'm amazed you are," Josette said.

"I'm much too excited to sleep. It's the last Sunday of my life as an unmarried woman."

"You're not having second thoughts, are you?"

"No. I can't wait to become Mrs. Bartholomew Parker Gordon."

"That's a mouthful, but you'll still just be Addison to me."

Addison handed Josette her coffee and then put hers on the nightstand near the opposite side of the bed. She stacked her pillows into a mound and shoved them against the headboard before climbing into bed next to Josette.

"Just like old times," Addison said. "Remember when we used to lie in bed on Sunday morning and give reviews of the previous night's date?"

"Yes, the good and the bad," Josette said. "Remember that jerk with the greasy hair who wanted to borrow ten dollars from me to pay his half of the cheap pizza?"

"Refresh my memory. Why did you ever go out with him in the first place?"

"He had a really cool car. But then do you remember that date you had with the guy who had to call his mother every few minutes all through the meal?"

"Who could forget? I figured we were going to have to stop by his house so she could burp him. She worried about him when he was out late, he claimed. It wasn't even ten o'clock."

They laughed their way through their coffee.

"So how are you and Keenan hitting it off?" Addison asked.

How much to tell? That she'd had a hard time sleeping last night remembering what it felt like to be held in his arms while dancing? That her body still tingled from his hand splayed across her back? She decided to keep that to herself. "He's nice," she said instead, "but I barely know him."

"Don't use that 'he's nice' routine with me. I invented it. Besides, I saw the two of you dancing last night. If you'd been any closer, he'd have been breathing through *your* nose."

She should have known she couldn't keep the truth from her best friend. She sighed out a breath. "Okay, so he's hot. And nice. And brave. He even met my dad yesterday and he survived that."

"So, all my worries about how you'd respond to an FBI agent were wasted?"

"I was worried about that myself, but he's been a real help."

"Is your dad okay?"

She shrugged. "Not really, but we are not going there this morning. Happy thoughts only for your wedding eve, remember? To change the topic, how did you know it was the real thing with Bart? Was it love at first sight?"

"Far from it. When Mother first started pitching him to me, I figured how exciting could a corporate attorney be? And my mother adored him. I felt she was pushing me at him, so that was another major turnoff."

"Poor Bart. How'd you overcome that?"

"We laughed a lot when we were together. About nothing. Dating got to be easy. Movies, hiking, kayaking, dancing. I knew things were going well, but I didn't know how well until he had to go out of town on business for a month."

"Absence worked, huh?"

"And how. Nothing went right while he was gone and then he walked back through the door and my world turned right again. He was everything I'd ever wanted in a man. I just never knew it until that minute."

She was truly happy for her friend. "Was it the same for Bart?"

"Not that he admits. He claims from the night he met me he knew I was the one."

"And now you're getting married. It all sounds so romantic."

"I'm sure the mechanics of it are different for everyone, but I think when it's love, you'll know it."

"You make it sound easy, Addison, but in my mind, I never connect love with marriage or with happy-ever-after. My parents were always in love, but marriage never worked for them. They were always going in opposite directions and wondering why they couldn't arrive at the same place."

Addison turned to face her squarely and looked her in the eyes. "You're not your mother or your father, Josette. Now enough about love. I'm hungry and the prerehearsal brunch at Mom's isn't until one." She jumped to her feet.

"We could go out for beignets," Josette suggested.

"We could or I was thinking we could invite the rest of the wedding party up to our balcony for a room service continental breakfast. Very informal. Dress code of pj's, hotel robe optional."

"How many do you think you can get to drag themselves out of bed this early after the ball last night?"

"My guess is two."

Josette could guess which two she meant. "I hate to put Keenan on the spot. I've taken up so much of his time already."

"Keenan is a big boy. He can say no if he wants to."

Josette threw off the covers. "When you put it that way, why not?"

KEENAN FINISHED HIS second cup from the pot of strong, chicory-laden coffee he'd ordered from room service. He'd spent a restless night, lying awake until after two and then stirring when the first rays of sunrise slanted through the blinds in his hotel room.

That was par for the course when he was on a difficult case. Problem was, this wasn't his case. He had no authority, no responsibility.

The longer he was with Josette, the more he picked up on her edginess. Despite how she tried to underplay it, she was worried her mother had met with foul play. And no matter how she tried to hide it, she was suspicious of her father's actions. His training had taught him well how to read people. Especially people he was getting to know.

Nothing about this case seemed to add up. Why was Antoine selling his boat? Who was the figure he chased on the bayou? Why was Detective Hyde investigating Antoine? What was Lorraine Cormier's angle in all of this?

Yeah, he thought, the case was getting under his skin.

And it wasn't all about Josette, either. He'd have jumped in and done what he could for anyone in her position. Well, he might not have jumped in quite as quickly for someone who hadn't already knocked his socks off.

The truth was he hadn't been with any woman since his leg had taken shrapnel from an unexpected explosion.

The pain and rehab had consumed him the first few weeks. But from the moment he'd met Josette on the flight, he'd felt the chemistry firing between them.

His cell phone rang. He reached for it, knocking his empty coffee cup off the bedside table in the process. He checked the caller ID. Bart.

"What's up, guy?"

"Nothing yet. That's the problem. Just waiting for the man who's supposed to be keeping me sane for the next two days to show up."

Keenan laughed at his friend's dry sense of humor. "Oh, yeah, that is my job, isn't it? Do you want to grab breakfast somewhere?"

"Right after I find a hair of the dog that bit me."

"Do the bars in New Orleans open this early?"

"I know one that does, and the price is right—at least for us."

"When and where?"

"Now, on the balcony of the Princess Suite."

Josette's room? "Was I invited?"

"Absolutely. The rest of the wedding party was, too, but according to Addison, one claimed morning sickness and the rest of them groaned, then no doubt rolled over and went back to sleep."

"I'll need a minute to throw on some clothes."

"Addison says dress code is pajamas, robes optional."

"Pajamas? Do men still wear those?"

"No one I know, except my dad. A pair of clean boxers will suffice just in case the robe comes open. I don't think they'd reward us with beads for flashing them."

"Might be worth a try. Meet you at their room in ten. Got to brush my teeth first. The taste of lobster and whiskey still lingers on the tongue."

"That could be because you ate a whole tray of those seafood canapés. But do brush, for all our sakes. See you in the suite."

Ten minutes later, Keenan was sitting on the balcony next to Josette, both in their robes. Her hair was damp, as if she'd just stepped out of a shower. Her skin was makeup free and as flawless as porcelain. He couldn't tell one scent from another, but he knew she smelled good enough to eat.

"Can you believe this weather?" Josette asked. "It's supposed to be in the high seventies by afternoon."

"If it holds through Mardi Gras, I'm sure the wilder costumes will show a lot of skin."

An older couple walked down the street below them holding hands. They waved as they approached the balcony. Keenan reached for one of the colorful, glass necklaces that draped the metal railing. He held it over the balcony and let it drop into the woman's upstretched hands.

"Happy Mardi Gras," she called as she slipped it around her neck.

A shop owner across the empty street swept the used to-go cups and trash from in front of his store, before piling it all into a large black bag.

"Mardi Gras must be rough on street cleaners," Josette said.

"The French Quarter takes its trash seriously," Keenan said. "I've read they measure the success of Mardi Gras by the number of tons of trash they collect."

"From what I've seen so far, this year will be a roaring success," Josette said. "But I love the calm ambiance this time of morning."

The bells from St. Louis Cathedral chimed, evoking a peaceful reverence. Keenan hoped that was a prelude to a day where the surprises were all centered around a perfect wedding weekend for Bart and Addison.

Addison opened the sliding glass door and joined them on the balcony. A waiter pushing a cart filled with scones, croissants, muffins, jam, a pot of coffee and a pitcher of orange juice followed her. Bart was a step behind them, balancing Bloody Marys on a round tray.

The four of them spent the next couple of hours nursing a drink or two, munching on muffins and talking about everything except Isadora and Antoine Guillory.

Keenan tried but couldn't keep his mind or his eyes off Josette. He battled the sensations rumbling inside him, knowing the pangs of desire were making it difficult to think clearly.

When he finally headed back to his room, his phone rang. It was Detective Max Hyde returning Keenan's call from yesterday afternoon. Keenan was surprised to hear back from him so quickly. He figured it was either a good sign that the detective was eager to get back to Josette or a worrisome sign that he had bad news to share.

"I got a message that Josette Guillory wanted to talk to me about the Isadora Guillory case," Max said after his introduction.

"Yes. We're only here for a few days. I know you're bound to be stressed during the festival, but if you could spare even a few minutes of your time, that would be great."

"It will be a very few minutes but there are a couple things I should clear up with Ms. Guillory. First, I need to know your identity and your relationship with Josette."

Keenan gave his name. "It's not really much of a relationship," he admitted. "Josette and I are both in town for a wedding, so I guess I only qualify as a concerned friend."

"Then you're not another detective she's hired?"

"No, but I may as well level with you. I'm an FBI agent in the counterterrorism division, currently on medical leave for rehab. Like I said, I'm just acting as a concerned friend in this situation." When Max was quiet, he added, "You can check that out. I'm not trying to interfere or usurp your authority in any way."

"Good," Max said. "Nice to get that straight up front. Before we go any further, we need to bring Josette in on this, as well. I'm crazy busy around here, but if you two can meet me now, I can see you for a few minutes."

"Where?" Keenan asked.

"You left me your hotel and room number. I could meet you both there in about ten minutes if Josette is agreeable with that."

"Actually, I left you *my* room number," he said, keeping it clear they weren't sharing a room.

"I'll check with Josette, but since I know how eager she is to meet with you, I think we're safe in setting up the meeting. My room, ten minutes from now. If it doesn't work for her, I'll get right back to you."

They might be wasting Max's time, but something about Josette's father's sudden urge to ditch the life he'd always known threw up red flags no investigator would ignore. He had an idea Hyde fell into that category.

If Max had any new info about Josette's mother, Keenan prayed it was good news.

Chapter Ten

Josette wiggled into a pair of jeans and a long-sleeved T-shirt. There was no time to bother with makeup, so she settled for a touch of lip gloss and running a comb through her hair.

By the time she got to Keenan's room, Detective Max Hyde was waiting. There were only two chairs in the room. Hyde was sitting in a leather swivel chair next to a hotel-style desk. Keenan motioned for her to take the upholstered armchair near the window.

Keenan dropped onto the edge of the unmade bed. His room was nice and spacious but didn't compare to the Princess Suite.

The plainclothes detective flicked a spot of lint off his slightly wrinkled jeans and ran his fingers through his short brown hair. He looked a little scruffy, as if he could use a shave and likely some sleep.

"Thanks for meeting with us on such short notice," she said.

"No problem. Glad we could hook up."

"Have you made any further progress toward locating my mother?"

The detective let out a breath, slowly. His words were measured when he spoke. "A year has passed. That in itself makes changes in any possible foul play situation."

"What exactly does that mean?"

"Just that the longer a case remains unsolved, the less likely it is to be solved. Of course, in Isadora's case, that doesn't necessarily add up that way."

"In what way?"

"Isadora has a pattern of disappearing over extended periods of time, only to appear when people least expect it. Or, rather, when it suits her career. I'm sure we went through all this when Isadora first disappeared. Yet, I never expected it to last this long."

"My father says you've been hanging around Alligator Cove asking a lot of questions of him and other locals. What is that about?"

Hyde crossed an ankle over his knee. "Are you sure you want to include Keenan Carter in this discussion?"

She flashed Keenan a quick glance, then looked squarely at the detective. "Yes," she said with confidence. "I value his input."

"Then I'll level with both of you. Four months ago I transferred from the NOPD missing persons department to Homicide, although I'm still following up on your mother's case."

At the word *homicide* her stomach roiled, and she suddenly wished she'd gone easier on the Bloody Marys earlier that morning. "Will you stay with the case?"

"For now, at least as far as I know." He lowered his leg to the floor and sat up straight, his gaze never wavering from Josette. "Two bodies have washed up in the bayou over the past eight months. Neither of the cases has been solved so investigations are becoming more intense."

"I'm sorry to hear that." She truly was. She'd always considered the Alligator Cove area one of the safest in the country—except for bayou-related accidents, of course.

"Not sure what you know about Alligator Cove, but the entire area has become a hotbed for feuding drug cartels. They're moving drugs into the area via the Gulf."

"Drugs." Keenan leaned forward and his eyes met Josette's and she nodded, giving him a silent command to tell the detective about yesterday. "There's another reason we called you, Detective." He told Hyde about the gunman he'd encountered in the bayou.

Hyde nodded. "Could be part of the drug cartel. Wherever they go, violence follows. Then again—"

Much as Josette wanted to get to the bottom of the bayou shooter, she was more concerned about her missing mother. "Detective, I hear what you're saying about these cartels, but I'm not sure what that has to do with my father or my mother. Neither of them would get involved in drugs."

"You're likely right," the detective agreed. "But it's not out of the realm of possibility that Isadora got caught in the wrong place at the wrong time. Maybe saw something she wasn't supposed to see."

"Did you ever determine if or how Isadora escaped this area after she disappeared?" Keenan asked.

"No. All I can say for certain is that if she left the country that night or anytime since by any commercial means, she used a fake passport."

"Which would be fairly easy enough for a woman with her money and connections to get," Keenan observed. "What about a chartered plane?"

"We checked that immediately. We got nowhere. No record of a passenger fitting her description leaving any airport in this area during the hours, days and weeks following her disappearance."

"Do you have a list of charters that left the area and claimed no passengers?" Keenan asked.

"Good question. We do, and we've questioned everyone involved with those flights. The FBI assisted in that part of the investigation."

"Mother always had connections that could get her a chartered flight at a moment's notice," Josette said. "She could easily buy their silence. Great for dodging the paparazzi, you see."

"Yes, you gave me the names of some pilots she'd used before, and they were thoroughly checked out."

"I gave you the ones I knew about," Josette corrected.

"What about a current money trail?" Keenan asked. "Are any of her bank accounts active?"

"The only money issue I see as relevant to the case right now is the five hundred thousand dollars Isadora had transferred from an account in New York to a bank in New Orleans. She withdrew that money last year once she arrived in the city."

"She also withdrew a large amount of cash the last time she left on one of her escapes," Josette said. "I know it seems like a lot of cash, but not to Isadora. Not when you consider the amount she'll splurge for a piece of jewelry, a shopping excursion or one time even a yacht."

"Still sounds like a lot of cash to be walking around with in this area, especially at Mardi Gras," Keenan noted.

"Mother was always surrounded by bodyguards."

"Not the morning she left the hotel before dawn," Hyde said.

"Did someone see her leave the hotel?" Keenan questioned.

"Not exactly. The back-door camera shows her leaving the hotel with one wheeled piece of luggage at seven minutes past 5 a.m. She walked to the side of the hotel, turned the corner and disappeared into the darkness. The general assumption is that she got into a waiting car that was just out of sight of the cameras. She was not seen again after that."

While that sounded like a modus operandi her mother would have used to escape, Josette realized it didn't prove her mother had gotten into a friendly car. She could just as easily have been pulled into a vehicle by someone meaning to do her harm.

Keenan stood and paced the room for a few seconds, obviously feeling as anxious as she was. "Did the security camera on her floor show her leaving the room?"

"Not exactly. The film was missing from the camera. It happens sometimes in this business. Not everyone wants a digital record of their comings and goings or who they were with."

"Did you get fingerprints from the camera?"

"We tried. There were none. Someone had wiped it clean. I know what you're thinking, but the hotel hallways are constantly cleaned."

Despite that, Josette felt her chest tighten. With every revelation, Max Hyde was poking holes in her long-held hope that her mother was off on one of her jaunts. She had been denying any other possibility. But now, how could she ignore the possibility that her mother had been the victim of foul play? Even with her bodyguard asleep in an adjoining room.

Keenan must have read the fear on her face. He placed a comforting hand on her shoulder. Just a touch as he paced by, but she took whatever strength she could from it.

"It's difficult to believe a woman who millions of people could recognize on sight could just vanish into thin air," he said.

"Believe me, the case has inspired countless conspiracy theories," the detective said. "Some of her fans are convinced she was captured by an alien or she's living with a vampire on Rampart Street. Another swears that Isadora had facial surgery that has made her unrecognizable to the paparazzi who refuse to let her have a personal life."

"What's your theory?" Keenan asked.

"I want to believe just like her fans do, that Isadora is alive and well, but I can't ignore the possibility that she might have been killed, not after a year has passed."

Hyde stood up and walked to the window, parting the drapes to look out onto Bourbon Street. "The French Quarter is extremely safe when you stick to the tourist areas. Unfortunately, there are still criminals around here who'd kill for a pair of sneakers and a whole lot more who'd kill for five hundred grand—if they knew she was carrying that kind of cash around."

"But where's the evidence?" Josette interjected, her fear and frustration obvious in her tone. "And even if there was, my father is positively not involved in it. If you're accusing him, can't you at least tell me that? You need to stop treating him like he's a suspect."

"I consider everyone a suspect until they're proven innocent," Hyde said. "That's my job." He checked his watch. "Until we arrest a suspect, your father and his friends and neighbors should expect to see even more of me."

"Why? What has changed? Mother has been missing for almost a year and you've never seemed to seriously consider Dad a suspect."

"The whole area has changed. When new people, places and events come into play, new information may work its way to the top. Money that was never up for grabs before suddenly jumps into the game."

Hyde's ambiguous remark confounded her. "Are you saying you're planning to arrest my father?"

"I'm saying, sometimes people start remembering things they haven't thought of in months." He started making his way to the door. "Look, Josette, talk to Antoine if you want, but my advice is that you stay away from your dad and his friends at Alligator Cove, especially with all the rumors circulating about deadly drug deals and money flowing in new directions."

She didn't have to worry about staying away from her father. He was doing a fine job of avoiding her.

Before Hyde stepped out, he said over his shoulder, "Danger can sometimes lurk in familiar places that seem safe. I'm sure Keenan can vouch for that." Then the door slammed shut behind him.

Keenan could, but he wouldn't, he decided. His words would be futile. There wasn't a chance in hell Josette would go back to Nashville now until she was satisfied she'd done what she could to get through to her father or gotten to the bottom of what happened with her mother.

But giving foul play a place at the head of the table highlighted a lot of dangerous concerns. Deadly secrets waiting to be exposed. Crimes creeping from the abyss of the forbidden past. Perilous enigmas.

If someone had killed Isadora Guillory for whatever reason, he—or she—might have reason to strike again if Josette got too close. Which was why Keenan pledged to stay near Josette until she let this go and flew back to Nashville.

Damn, he didn't want to think about her leaving under any circumstances. He'd never fallen for a woman this quick or this hard in his life.

The injury to his leg would likely pale compared to the injury to his heart when she walked out of his life.

Assuming he could keep her safe till then.

JOSETTE CALLED HER DAD. She needed to ask him some questions, not the least of which was why he had packed luggage. Where was he planning to go? No answer. She decided a quick walk in the brisk Sunday morning air might help clear her mind.

The carnival spirit was buzzing everywhere. Musicians, mimes, balloon artists entertained the tourists.

A stream of people were leaving the beautiful St. Louis Cathedral and hitting the streets along Jackson Square. Dozens of coffee seekers had already formed lines to get into the patio seating at Café du Monde.

An elderly man stopped and slipped a colorful string of beads around her neck and wished her happy Mardi Gras. A woman hummed as she set up her easel, readying her prime spot for gaining the attention of new portrait subjects.

A crowd gathered, their feet tapping to the beat as a talented young man played, "When the Saints Go Marching In" on his trumpet. Josette listened for a few minutes and then dropped a tip into the hat that was lying upside down in front of him.

It was a great morning to be on the streets of the Vieux Carré. Not a frown in sight, except for her own.

She picked up her pace and returned to her room

just in time to shower and dress for the Landrys' brunch. Her phone rang as she added a final sweep of blush along her cheeks. It was Addison.

"Josette. Where are you, girl?"

"I went for a walk to work up an appetite, but I'm dressed and ready to go. Where are you?"

"In the lobby with Sara, Beth and some of my cousins. Our limo is supposed to be here any minute now."

"I'll be right down."

"Great. Can you bring the sequined clutch I left on the table in the sitting area? It's small, just big enough to hold a mirror and lipstick."

She stepped into the room. "I see it. Meet you in the lobby in two."

Josette squeezed into a crowded elevator, then stole a few seconds to see if the envelope from Celeste Rubenstein had arrived. The clerk assured her it hadn't.

By the time Josette located Addison and the others, the limo was waiting. It was at least a half hour later before they reached the Landrys' St. Charles Avenue mansion. The live oak tree–lined streets were full of paradegoers staking out their spots on the parade route. The limo driver had to let them out on a side street a short walk away.

The ornate double doors to the beautiful home were open, yet clusters of guests were enjoying the beautiful weather with cocktails in hand on the wide, covered veranda.

Addison stopped to visit with several of the guests, introducing Josette, Sara and Beth to a new round of friends and family. A young man with a tray of drinks approached Josette and the others as they stepped inside the beautiful marble foyer.

Josette, Sara and Addison chose flutes of cranberry mimosas. Beth opted to wait for water which the young man went immediately to the bar to get for her.

"Nice," Sara said as he walked away.

"The mimosa?" Beth asked.

"No, the waiter's buns. Surely you haven't been married so long that you no longer notice?"

"I notice. I just don't drool the way you do."

Sara scoffed. "Only because you're married to your prince."

"Just so you know, the waiter is available," Addison interjected. "He works for the catering company Mother uses for large gatherings and is also working on a PhD in biomedical engineering."

"Way too brainy for me," Sara said on an exaggerated sigh.

"Can't you tell she's looking for a jock like Moose?" Beth teased. "They were smoking hot on the dance floor last night."

Sara smiled mischievously "Just getting to know each other."

They took their drinks to the spacious family room. A group of white-haired women loaded down with Mardi Gras beads were demonstrating their very impressive second-line movements and laughing so hard, Josette figured their near-empty champagne flutes were not the first of the day.

Addison waved at them. They waved back and motioned her over.

"I see Aunt Louise and her bridge buddies are already getting warmed up for the reception tomorrow night," Addison said. "I need to say hello. Save me a place at your table once you've visited the buffet. I have a little presentation to make to my wonderful attendants."

"And don't let me forget to give you the something borrowed I promised to lend you," Josette said.

"What in the world are you lending her?" Sara said. "Addison has absolutely everything."

"I bet it's those gorgeous earrings Josette's mother brought her back from Florence," Beth said.

"You'll have to wait and see." Josette scanned the room, looking for Keenan, though she didn't want to admit that even to herself. She spotted him with Moose and Lance talking to a group of guys over by the stone fireplace, one of five in the three-story house. None were needed today.

Josette could hear just enough of their conversation to know they were talking about football. It might be an hour or more before he stopped to eat.

"Am I the only one that those fabulous odors are getting to?" Beth asked. "I'm starving."

"I could eat," Josette admitted.

"Let's grab a table and reserve it out with our handbags," Beth suggested. "Inside or outside? From previous parties at the Landrys', I'm sure there are choices on the back terrace, the garden or the pool."

"Definitely outside," Beth said. "I won't have those choices when I get back to Montana. Just talked to John. It's snowing there as we speak."

They chose a table set for four in the gardens on the east side of the house and then headed to the dining room.

Josette stared in awe. She'd partaken of amazing spreads at the Landry home before, but nothing quite this elaborate. This was fit for royalty—or more specifically the wedding preliminaries for their only daughter.

Addison's mother was standing near the abundance of beautiful desserts that covered one of the oversize sideboards. Another held platters of fruits, cheeses, boiled shrimp and a half dozen different salads.

Mrs. Landry walked over and went down the row hugging each of them. "It's so great to have you all here together again. You can't imagine how Whelan and I have missed those weekends you spent here before you graduated and ran off to distant lives. Now we barely even see Addison and she lives here in town."

Tears moistened Mrs. Landry's eyes.

"Forgive me," she said. "I'm thrilled Addison has found someone as wonderful as Bart. It's just that…" She sniffled and pulled a dainty handkerchief from her pocket and dabbed her eyes. "Weddings are tough on mothers."

That called for another round of hugs.

"The wedding will be the start of a new family for you to love," Beth sympathized. "My mother hated losing me to John, but now that I'm pregnant, all she can talk about is having a grandbaby. Suddenly, no plane ride is too long."

"You're pregnant? I hadn't heard," Mrs. Landry gushed. "I'm so happy for you *and* your mother." She teared up again.

"Did you prepare all of this food yourself?" Josette asked, changing the subject. It was going to be a long day for Mrs. Landry if she broke into tears with everyone at the brunch.

"I had a lot of the food catered, but I made a few of the dishes myself, like the seafood crepes you used to love so much, Beth."

Beth rubbed her hands together. "Well, that's my lunch. I'm skipping everything else so I can pig out on those."

"Apparently, just the thought of them cures morning sickness," Sara teased.

"Shh," Beth warned. "Don't let my stomach hear that. It might take it as a challenge."

"I can give you the recipe, if you want," Mrs. Landry volunteered.

"You did, back when we were still at LSU. I never conquered it, and it would be difficult to get that variety of fresh seafood in Montana on any given day."

"I didn't think about that. I did think of Josette and Sara, though. Creole grits and grillades for Josette and seafood gumbo for Sara."

"I did finally learn to make grits and grillades," Josette said, "but they are never as good as yours."

"You're too kind."

A line had begun to form at the buffet. Mrs. Landry was quickly drawn into a new conversation.

Sara, Beth and Josette filled their plates to overflowing and settled in at their table. Addison joined them a few minutes later though her plate held nothing but small chunks of fresh fruit. She claimed to be too excited to eat. The rest of them dived in.

Once they were stuffed, Addison gave them their bridesmaid gifts, beautiful drop earrings with a single silver heart. The something borrowed from Josette was an exquisite diamond and sapphire ring that Isadora had given her on her eighteenth birthday.

It had spent most of its life in a safe. Expensive diamonds had never fit Josette's lifestyle, but success and happiness had always been measured in extravagance and celebrity status to Isadora.

Josette's phone rang. She lifted it from the outside pocket of her handbag and checked the ID.

"It's my dad," she said. "Can you excuse me? I've been waiting for his call, and I really need to take it."

"No apologies needed," they all assured her. She stood and walked down the garden path until she was out of earshot of any of the guests.

"Hi, Dad. I'm glad you called back. I really want to get together again before I fly back to Nashville."

"Why waste your time driving back down here? I'm busy. You're here for a wedding. Enjoy it."

She needed to talk to him. About so many things. She settled on the most innocuous. "I'm afraid you're making a huge mistake in selling your boat. After what you told me about Mother, I can't help but think she's behind that decision."

"I told you that Isadora has nothing to do with it. Or maybe she does, but not directly."

"Then how?"

"Your mother never hesitates to jump into new adventures. Maybe it's time I had an adventure or two myself."

"I just worry that you'll do something you'll regret later."

"I've made a lifetime of mistakes, Josette. I'm trying to right some of those now. I love you, but I have to do this my way. I hoped you'd understand."

"I'm trying, Dad. Let me drive down to see you Tuesday morning. Maybe we can go shrimping."

"I'll be busy. How about the FBI guy you were with?"

"He's not with me as an FBI guy."

"All the same, he seemed to be mighty stuck on you. Spend the day with him and stay completely away from here."

"But—"

"Laissez les bons temps rouler."

He issued the Cajun wish for her to let the good times roll and then broke the connection without giving her a chance to argue her point further. She felt a hand on her arm. Keenan. Her breath caught.

"Are you okay?" he asked.

"I've been better. That was Dad on the phone. I can't figure out what's going on with him. I told him I was coming back to see him on Fat Tuesday. He said not to come. He's never discouraged me from visiting before this trip."

"Isn't going to see him exactly what Detective Hyde warned you about?"

"It's what I have to do."

Keenan put an arm around her waist. "For what it's worth, I think you should take the detective's recommendations and at least for now stay clear of anything to do with Alligator Cove or the bayou in general."

That was just what her father said. "I probably should."

"But you're going anyway?"

She nodded.

"Well, then, it looks like I'll be on the bayou on Fat Tuesday."

"But you have a flight home."

"Not anymore. I canceled it."

"When?"

"This morning after the detective told you to go home and stay out of the way of the investigation. I knew before he got the words out of his mouth that you were going to ignore him."

"It's not that I'm unreasonable," she insisted.

"No. Stubborn, but not totally unreasonable. Still, someone has to keep you safe. Who better for that task than a temporarily out-of-work FBI agent?"

"Are you sure you want to get that involved?"

"Let's just say I'm not going anywhere until we leave this town together. Well, unless you report me as a stalker."

And suddenly she knew it was time to fully trust Keenan.

Chapter Eleven

Josette trusted Keenan in a way she'd never trusted any man before. She could look at him and feel passion stirring her soul. She could hear his voice and ache to have him take her in his arms.

He was her last thought before she closed her eyes at night and the sweetness that lingered on her lips until morning.

He was as close to real love as her heart could grasp. It was time to level with him, even if she did have to keep a few of her dad's secrets to herself.

A soft breeze caught loose tresses of Josette's long hair, blowing them across her face. Keenan raked them back and tucked them behind her ears. His fingers lingered briefly along the smooth column of her neck.

As always, his touch affected her senses, heating her insides, tripping along her nerves. She took a deep breath and exhaled slowly, seeking to ease the desire that wouldn't let go of her.

He captured that breath as he leaned down to kiss her. He held her in his burning hands, turning her head to deepen the kiss. When his tongue met hers, she knew it had been worth the wait. Kissing Keenan was unlike anything she'd ever experienced. Desire coiled within her and she'd have given anything to be somewhere she could show him just what he'd come to mean to her.

Reluctantly she stepped back, leaving only a breath between them. But she knew now was the time for a full confession.

"I need to share a few secrets with you, Keenan. Secrets that are tearing me apart but that I'm not totally free to share with just anyone."

"I'm glad you don't think of me as just anyone, Josette. At least we've gotten that far." He took both of her hands in his and his heated stare locked with hers. "You know I'll do anything I can to help you work through this, Josette, but I can't make that promise without establishing criteria."

"What criteria?"

"If you tell me something that involves breaking the law or withholding the truth from law enforcement personnel, I'd have to go to Detective Hyde or the FBI."

"I'd expect you to," she said, knowing his level of honesty was one of the main reasons she could trust him so blindly.

With a glance around them to make sure they were alone, she told him almost everything. Her father's warning, his packed bags, her every suspicion.

"He says selling the boat has to do with an 'adventure,' but I know it has to do with Isadora. Every decision he's ever made has. Why else would he not want anyone to know he's selling the boat and planning to leave the area?"

"Not even Detective Hyde?"

"Especially not Detective Hyde."

Furrows dug into Keenan's forehead. "Do you think that it's possible that Antoine has been in touch with Isadora himself and they're planning to rendezvous somewhere?"

"Anything's possible with Dad and Isadora. If that's true, he's likely setting himself up for another broken heart, and I'd hate to see that happen again. But once Dad makes up his mind to do something, he's cringeworthy stubborn."

"So that's where you get it from."

And then as if to make sure she knew he wasn't complaining, he pulled her into his arms and kissed her until she had to come up for air.

She could no longer deny that she might be cruising for a broken heart. But it might be worth it.

IT WAS MIDAFTERNOON. Clouds piled in the sky like fluffy puffs of whipped cream. The birds sang in the breeze. Frogs croaked as if they owned the surrounding area, and blackbirds chattered to defend their own territory.

Antoine felt like making that same noisy chatter, a complaint that his world had been disrupted.

Try as he might, Antoine couldn't get his heartbeat to regulate. What were the odds this would all resolve his way? He understood the demands, accepted the terms, and now there was nothing else to do but wait.

Waiting for the signs of proof that Isadora was safe and on the way home.

But could he trust a kidnapper's demands?

A kidnapper who held the life of his beloved Isadora in his hands. And Antoine's life, too.

Two more days, he thought. In two days this would all be over. On Tuesday, Isadora would be his again… or the agony would continue.

No, he had to believe it would work. And it would work—if he could keep Josette and her snooping FBI agent away.

For now, he had a few more things to do to get ready.

He was almost back to his house when he heard an approaching vehicle. He quickly realized that it was Daniel behind the wheel of the dirty SUV. He felt both relief and disillusion. He wouldn't take an easy breath until this whole dangerous and chaotic situation was over and done with.

Sure that Daniel was here to complain about not getting to buy the shrimp boat, Antoine made a seat of the top few steps.

"I'm really sorry, Daniel," he said as the young man approached, "but the *Lady Isadora* is sold."

"I know," he replied, nearly spitting out the words. "But that's not why I'm here." He remained standing, looking down at Antoine. It concerned Antoine that he couldn't read anything but hatred in Daniel's expression.

The young man's eyes narrowed to slits. "I don't know exactly what's going on, Antoine, but I know enough to know someone else is calling the shots for you."

Antoine's chest tightened but he forced a calm demeanor. "Do you want to explain that?"

"There were a few drunks at the table in the back corner of the crab shack. The more they drank, the mouthier they got. Don't think they knew I could hear them since I was in and out of the kitchen."

"Go on, Daniel," Antoine encouraged.

"They mentioned a hit by the cartel. That's all I heard, except when I swung by again I heard them say Guillory Road."

"Did they name anybody?"

"Nope." He took off his cap and wiped the sweat from his brow. He speared Antoine with a sharp look. "You involved with them cartels?"

Antoine nearly laughed. Ironic. He was involved with unsavory types, all right, but not the cartel. "No, Daniel. Despite whatever's going on between us, you know me better."

He replaced his cap. "Probably just their beer talking but I figure somebody ought to know."

"Why don't you pass it along to Detective Hyde. He's here often enough."

He was the one thing Antoine wouldn't miss when he was gone.

It was five in the evening when the wedding party and guests finished the rehearsal activities in a delightful French Quarter courtyard, ablaze with huge pots of spring flowers. The wedding itself would be tomorrow evening in the beautiful St. Louis Cathedral, but for now everyone seemed to scatter at once using their last spurt of free time before the wedding.

Some headed to a rock concert at House of Blues. Others went to catch the Bacchus parade or stayed in town to throw or catch a few more beads. Josette encouraged Keenan to go with one of the livelier groups, but he'd said his leg was starting to complain.

It did seem as if the limp was more pronounced than it had been that morning, but she doubted he'd have gone without her if he'd been pain free.

The attraction between them was intensifying at a dangerous pace, at least it was on her part. She was fairly sure he felt the same, though neither had put those feelings into words.

They were walking through the hotel's guarded door when Josette spotted Harley Broussard walking out. Their gazes met and he quickly turned and started speed-walking away from the hotel. Turning away from Keenan, she went back through the door and caught up with him before he could disappear into the crowds on the street. She grabbed his arm and tugged him to a stop.

"Why are you avoiding me, Harley? This is the second time you walked away without speaking."

"Sorry, Josette. I wasn't avoiding you. I just wasn't sure that was you. It's been a while."

"Not that long," she countered.

Keenan joined them, breathing heavily as he ran to her side.

"Keenan, this is Harley Broussard, one of my dad's

neighbors and according to my dad, a born shrimper. He worked for Dad some when he was in high school."

"Good to meet you, Harley." He introduced himself, but he couldn't stop looking at Josette. She figured he knew there was something bothering her about this man.

Harley acknowledged the greeting with more of a grunt than a comment and turned away. "Good to see you, Josette, but no time to visit. I'm meeting friends."

Josette grabbed his forearm to keep him in place. "Are you staying at this hotel?" she asked, not willing to let him escape so quickly.

Harley shook his head. "Too rich for my blood. Super nice hotel, though."

"This is the second time I've seen you here," she pointed out.

"Do you work here?" Keenan asked.

"Not anymore. I used to work here, part-time on occasions when they were extremely busy, like now. I've still got friends who work here so I hang out here some."

"Were you working here when Isadora Guillory went missing?" Keenan questioned.

He hesitated a second before answering. "Unfortunately, yes."

"That must have caused quite a commotion."

"You got that right," Harley agreed.

"Tell us about it," Keenan prompted him.

Harley seemed to think for a second, then he volunteered the information. "I've never seen anything like it. Reporters, photographers and cops hanging out all over the place. Outnumbered the guests."

"Did you see my mother before she went missing?" Josette asked.

"From a distance, but there was no way to get near her. If the paparazzi weren't chasing her down like a pack of wolves, her fans were doing it for them. Bodyguards were worth twice what she was paying them."

"Isadora must have been frightened," Keenan said.

"Nope. The bodyguards, maybe, but not Isadora. As soon as they cleared the worst of the shoving masses out of her way, she started waving and blowing kisses to her fans."

Keenan stepped closer to Harley. "Then you never talked to Isadora during her stay?"

"A working peon like me? Security would have thrown me out in a second if I'd gotten anywhere near her."

"Security must have been all over the place," Keenan said.

"You know it. It was Mardi Gras week, like now. Every room was booked, and Isadora wasn't the only TV star here. There were several I didn't recognize. And then there was Grant Gaines."

"The costar?" Keenan questioned.

"Right. He thought he was a real big shot. He had women half his age and twice his age chasing after him like he was a rock star instead of some nighttime soap hack."

"Were you on duty when they realized Isadora was missing?" Keenan asked.

"Yeah, but I was working room service. Didn't find out what was really going on until it hit the news." He poked his hands in his front pockets and rattled his keys. "Look, Josette, I'm real sorry about your mother, but you know how she was. I mean nice enough, but a kook and a snob. Always too good for any of us who lived in or around Alligator Cove."

"Mother might not have fit in, but she wasn't a snob," Josette defended.

"Well, whatever. I gotta go. Like I said, meeting some friends and I'm running late." He turned on his heel and walked away before Josette had time to stop him.

"I'd say your bayou buddy there knows more than he's saying," Keenan remarked as they watched Harley meld into the throng of revelers.

"What makes you think that?"

"Lack of eye contact with either one of us. Nervously shifting his weight. Perspiration on his forehead even though the air is turning cooler. There are dozens of clues if you know what to look for."

And, of course, Keenan would. But what could Harley possibly know that Detective Hyde and the persistent media, plus all her experienced detectives, didn't?

"I'm going to stop at the front desk and see if Celeste left the thumb drive of photos," Josette said. "Not that I know what I'm looking for."

"Don't underestimate yourself. Many a case has been solved by a seemingly insignificant element that went unnoticed at first."

"Even after a year?"

"Even after decades."

This time the thumb drive was waiting for her at the hotel desk.

"Showtime at my place or yours?" Keenan asked.

"Mine has a sofa you can stretch your leg out on and I'm sure my roommate will be out for at least another couple of hours."

"You sold me. I'll bring my computer."

JOSETTE WAITED AS Keenan set up the computer and started the slideshow. The first dozen or so photos were of the krewe's officers and others recognized for outstanding service to the krewe throughout the year.

The next few highlighted the food, the band and the decorations. After that there were dozens of candid shots of the members and guests at the ball.

They were about ten minutes into the slideshow when Josette spotted the shimmering, backless ball gown and the long, auburn hair.

Her breath caught as she stared at the picture and a cold shiver crawled along her nerve endings. "Pause it," she murmured. "The woman in the glittering, slinky dress is Isadora."

Chapter Twelve

Keenan stared at the picture. "She's as stunning as I've heard, especially in that gown."

"That's one of my original designs, created especially for her."

"Do you know the people clustering around her?"

"No, but Isadora probably didn't know them, either, before that night. She was always surrounded by fans and admirers wherever she went."

Keenan forwarded to the next picture, a side view of Isadora. The profile shot offered an even better view of the dress that clung to her svelte body and the slit that revealed one fabulous leg. She appeared to be staring into the eyes of a guy with movie star good looks, and an intriguing sprinkling of salt and pepper at his temples.

"Is that one of her cast members?" Kennan asked.

"Not one that I've ever seen before."

Keenan clicked, saving that picture to a new file.

"Any particular reason why you did that?" Josette asked.

"We may want to check the man out later. I don't

mean to insinuate anything about your mother, but Mardi Gras is known for encouraging people to release their inhibitions. If they hooked up later that night, he could know something that would help us."

"To be honest, Mother wasn't beyond hooking up with a guy she'd just met."

Josette regretted the words the second they left her mouth. Who was she to judge? Keenan might be thinking something very similar about her. She'd latched on to him fast enough.

They ran the slideshow slowly until they came to another photo of her mother. In this one she was signing autographs for a group of obviously excited women. Josette recognized some of them from last night's ball.

They moved through a few more snapshots before stopping at another one.

"So much for Mr. Gorgeous," Keenan said. "Isadora looks just as enthralled by the guy she's dancing with in this picture."

"That's her costar Grant Gaines. This was a publicity trip and her fans love believing there was an authentic chemistry between the two of them. Either good or bad, the interactions kept the sensual tension high for the show."

"Have they been lovers in the past?"

"Difficult to know when they were both so good at living in their make-believe world. They were convincingly hot and heavy a couple of years back—before they became so competitive with every aspect of the show."

"You told me before they competed for the most screen time and the biggest paycheck. Who won the bragging rights?"

"Mother, by far. Needless to say, he's winning this season since Mom has at least been temporarily written out of the series."

The slideshow kept running. On the last photo Keenan paused it. Isadora and Grant were alone in the picture, though obviously the photographer had them in his viewfinder. The couple were on the balcony apparently having anything but a loving conversation. Her hands were at her hips, her face twisted in anger. His torso was leaning into her in a threatening position.

"That was a quick turnaround," Keenan said.

"Typical of Mother and Grant. Their moods can swing without a second's warning. Always have."

"Was Grant investigated after Isadora disappeared? Did he have an alibi?"

Josette dragged her eyes from the screen and looked at him. "He was. I remember the police saying Grant claimed he was passed out somewhere. I can't remember where. Now I figure it was too much partying at this ball."

Keenan looked back at Grant in the photo. The man looked stone-cold sober. And he looked angry. At Isadora.

Grant Gaines just made it to the top of his suspect list.

As soon as he could, he'd have Dwayne run a check on the actor.

"Have you seen enough?" Keenan asked. "Or do you want to go through them again?"

"I've had enough for now. I'm not sure the pictures helped, but it was worth the trouble just to see my mother laughing and dancing and enjoying herself—until she wasn't. I keep trying to tell myself that she's alive now, but Detective Hyde certainly threw a wet blanket over that theory."

"That's the way with investigators," Keenan said. "Hope for the best, prepare for the worst. It's a curse of the job."

He closed his computer. "Do you want to sit on the balcony awhile, toss beads and soak in some uninhabited madness?"

"I'll pass on that for now, get some rest and hopefully wake up in a more positive mood for Addison and Bart's big day. The last thing I want to do is fall asleep at the altar in the beautiful, historic St. Louis Cathedral."

"Four years at LSU in Baton Rouge and dozens of trips to the French Quarter and I've never even seen the inside of that cathedral," Keenan admitted.

"It's magnificent. I can't imagine walking down the aisle and saying my vows in a place so holy and splendid."

Even sadder, Josette couldn't imagine walking down any aisle and repeating marriage vows anywhere, which made this whole sizzling attraction to Keenan even more difficult to grasp.

It had to be the situation. A perfect, romantic wedding between lovers. His help assuaging her growing concern for both her parents.

"I still have to come up with a befitting toast for the reception," Keenan said. "I can't get by on old football antics on such a grand occasion. Well, not more than once, anyway."

She walked him to the hallway door and opened it.

"Sweet dreams," Keenan murmured. "No thoughts of Detective Hyde or shrimp boats allowed."

"Good night, Keenan."

He leaned against the doorframe and lingered. "Did I tell you how beautiful you looked today, especially this morning on the balcony?"

"With wet hair, no makeup and a baggy robe?"

"Yep. You were completely mesmerizing."

A slow burn rode her senses.

Keenan trailed a finger down her face and across her lips, then leaned in closer.

A primal hunger exploded inside her. She knew she should close the door now, but passion melted her inhibitions. No longer able to fight the desire, she slipped her arms around his neck.

His lips found hers and that was it. She lost herself in the exhilaration, drowned in the passion racing through her body.

His breath mingled with hers as his tongue slipped between her lips. He ravaged her mouth so intensely, driving her until she could barely breathe.

When he finally pulled away, she was shaking, dizzy with the thrill of him. Her whole body ached for more, but if they didn't stop now, she'd lose all control.

When he leaned in again, she gave him a gentle shove in the chest.

"Time to go."

"If you insist." He squeezed her hand and then stepped away.

"Thanks for everything," she whispered. She closed the door quickly before she gave in to temptation and tugged him back inside. If she did, kisses would never be enough.

Chapter Thirteen

Josette woke as the first glow of daylight fought its way through the gray cloak of dawn. Her first thoughts were of Keenan. Impulsively, she touched her fingertips to her lips and the sweet memories reverberated through every cell in her body.

This was not her. Every romantic relationship she'd let herself be in before had developed slowly. Ever cautious, she'd weighed the pros and cons sensibly, never took risks with her heart.

It was a survival technique she'd learned from watching her parents destroy each other with the love they could never make work or give up on.

So why was it so different with Keenan? Did it even matter at this point in her life? Perhaps it was time she gave up on trying to control her every emotion.

Her mother had vanished. Her dad had basically become a stranger, one who was ready to walk away from the life he'd always loved.

Josette was losing all sense of normalcy.

There was no reason to think Keenan was forever, no assurance or even a hint that she'd see him again after the wedding.

Yet his touch was practically orgasmic. His kiss took her to levels of sexual arousal she'd never imagined.

Surely, a woman would have to be a fool to say no thank you to that.

THE WEDDING DAY agenda was packed, starting with ten o'clock appointments for manis and pedis at the hotel spa for Addison, Josette, Beth and Sara. Mimosas flowed freely in their private spa room for four.

Beth, of course, avoided the alcohol completely and munched on dry crackers. Fortunately, she claimed the nausea was manageable this morning.

Addison slipped her bare feet into the pedicure bowl. "I can't believe it's finally here. I also can't believe how exhausting all the planning was, but now that the big day is here, it was all worth it."

"So you're not sorry you didn't elope?" Beth teased.

"No, but there were days…"

"I'd never elope," Sara said. "Too easy to back out at the last minute. If I ever get married, I expect all three of you to be there to support me."

"I'll bring my baby with me to create chaos," Beth said.

"Your baby will be in school—maybe LSU—by the time I tie the knot," Sara said. "I have a lot of frogs left to kiss."

Addison laughed. "Then I guess the bouquet I toss tonight will need to have your name on it, Josette."

Josette shook her head. "My hands will be in my pocket."

"There are no pockets in that slinky silk gown you'll

be wearing," Beth reminded her. "There's hardly any room for a thong."

"Do you think our gowns are too seductive?" Josette asked.

"Absolutely," Beth said. "That's why I love them. I swear if it had balloon sleeves or a bow under the bustline I would have found some way to get out of this. Not sure Keenan's and Moose's hearts can take it as sexy as they are now, but that's their problem."

"Speaking of the guys, where are they off to this morning?" Josette asked.

"Bart arranged a real treat for them, and for himself," Addison said. "They drove over to LSU to have breakfast with the football coaching staff, most of whom were there all four years that the guys played."

"Lots of luck on them getting back in time for the wedding," Sara said.

"They'll be back," Addison assured her. "No wedding, no honeymoon in Italy."

By the time the second round of mimosas was poured, this one wisely weakened with an ample amount of orange juice, they were deep into reminiscing of their own college days.

"Okay," Addison said. "Best kisser, confined to the time we were all in school together."

"Easy for you three," Beth said. "I only seriously dated like four guys the whole time."

"No way, but let me guess," Josette said. "Robert Bailey."

"No." Beth shook her head. "He was never much in the sex department. He was a great tennis partner, though."

Sara snapped her fingers. "I got it. Brian Nash."

"Right on," Beth said. "Too bad he was lousy at tennis. What about you, Josette?"

"Geez. I hate these hard questions." Now if they'd extended the cutoff until today, this would be easy. Not that she'd kiss and tell. "I'll have to go with Michael Jennings," Josette said. "Senior year, on the golf team. He's a pro now."

"At kissing?" Beth asked.

"Could be. You'd have to ask his wife to get verification on that. He married Lana Rhodes, head Golden Girl."

By the time they were drying their fingernails under the heat lamp, Josette was feeling more relaxed than she had since arriving in New Orleans. This was what she'd come for, the uplift she always got when she was with this group.

She debated going back to her room and calling her dad but decided against it. It would only upset her and irritate him. Tomorrow would be soon enough for that.

The hotel staff served them a light lunch by the outdoor pool. The weather had held out. High temperature in the midseventies. Not even a chance of rain in the forecast.

A perfect day for a wedding.

"ARE YOU NERVOUS?" Keenan asked, trying to fulfill his best-man duties before they took their places for the wedding procession to begin.

"I haven't had time. I think one of the wedding

planner's main duties is to keep us too occupied to panic."

"More likely it's because you're marrying your best friend," Moose said.

"She is, you know," Bart said. "Any day that doesn't start and end with Addison in my arms isn't complete."

"If that's not the real thing, I don't know what is," Kennan said.

Until the last few days, he wouldn't have believed those words could have possibly come from his mouth. Josette had literally turned his world upside down in the most exciting way.

The first strains of the organ filled the awe-inspiring cathedral. The men took their places as the grandparents and parents of the bride and groom were led to their places on the second row of the nave. The first row remained empty.

The priest took his place as did Bart.

An adorable flower girl half skipped, half danced her way down the aisle dropping snowy white petals and tugging on the ring bearer's arm when he failed to keep up with her.

The two bridesmaids came next, followed by the maid of honor. Keenan's pulse began to race as he waited for his first glimpse of Josette. When she stepped onto the aisle, a million sensations hit at once, so strong he struggled for a reviving breath. It wasn't the awesome gown that had his heart racing. It was Josette.

He'd been intrigued with her the minute he saw her on the flight from Nashville. Before that night was over, he'd been enchanted with her. But it was her kisses and even her touch that had totally cratered him. Seeing her now, stunning, smiling despite all she was dealing with, only further crystalized his feelings for her.

The wedding was the most inspiring ceremony Keenan had ever witnessed, yet still his mind kept wandering back to the mystery surrounding Isadora's disappearance.

There were dozens of reasons to believe she had pulled off another successful disappearing act. Dozens more to suspect she was planning her surprise return.

But there were far too many suspects with a motive to kill Isadora for Keenan not to at least suspect that she could have been the victim of foul play.

Greed: Anyone who knew how much cash she was carrying on her the night before the disappearance.

Envy: Grant Gaines, a costar with a grudge against her.

Jealousy: Lorraine Cormier, eager to clear the way for her to marry Antoine.

Keenan mentally checked back into the ceremony as Addison and Bart were pronounced man and wife.

He and Josette marched out of the cathedral behind the newlyweds. The remainder of the wedding party, friends, family and guests joined the procession through the massive doors and then passing by Jackson Square on the way to the reception at the Jaxson Riverview Room.

Keenan's phone began to vibrate as they crossed

Decatur Street toward the old Jax Brewery. He left it
in his pocket, hoping the call was not more bad news
for Josette. There was no reason why it should be, but
his instincts were sending him bad vibes.

He excused himself when they reached the venue,
walked out onto the river-view terrace and checked
his messages.

The most recent one was from Detective Max Hyde.
This couldn't be good.

He returned the detective's call.

He was right. It wasn't good. It might just be the
worst possible development for Josette. There was
nothing they could do about it for a few more hours,
so there was no use in ruining the remainder of the
beautiful, moonlit evening.

The frightening news could wait until the reception was done and the bride and groom had left on
their honeymoon.

THE WEDDING CEREMONY had been magnificent, holy,
beautiful and poetic. Josette had fought back tears
more than once, especially when she'd looked at
Addison's mother, who'd occasionally broken into
sobs. There was so much love in the Landry family.

That was when reality had punched Josette in the
gut. She might not have her mother or her father at
her wedding—if there ever was a wedding.

The determined photographer had become a dic-
tator ever since they'd entered the reception venue.
He'd called for one grouping after another. Josette had
stayed out of the way as much as she could.

"Let's have the bride and her attendants only now," the eager, young photographer announced.

"Okay but I think we have enough posed shots of the guys," Addison said. "If we don't release them soon to join the feast, we may have a rebellion on our hands."

"That's what I'm talking about," Moose chimed in. "If I don't jump in quick, they're liable to run out of those fresh-shucked oysters."

"And the line at the bar is getting longer instead of shorter," Lance added.

The men happily joined the partying wedding guests after their one last posed group shot. After that, Addison insisted it was time for the bride to join the fun. There would be plenty more candid photo ops over the next few hours.

Josette went off to find Keenan. She hadn't had a chance to be alone with him since the mind-boggling kiss they'd shared last night. She couldn't help but wonder if he was experiencing the same tumultuous thrill that she was.

Was he eager to start where they'd left off or was he regretting that they were moving so quickly?

She took a flute of champagne from a passing waiter and then found Keenan walking away from the bar with a glass in hand.

"I thought I might find you near the bar," she said as she approached him.

"Yeah. I handled the wedding fine, but I thought the photographer was never going to finish."

"I'm sure he's nowhere close to finished, but the worst of it is over. What are you drinking?"

"Scotch on the rocks."

"I thought you were a beer man," Josette said.

"I usually am but this is a special occasion, and they have premium double malt Scotch. Besides, I need fortification to get through my required tasks. I've been known to flub a toast or two."

"I have a feeling few would notice at a party this loud and lavish."

"You could be right. Would you like a cocktail?"

"Not yet. I'll stick with champagne for now."

They took their drinks and made their way to the head table, squeezing into the seats with their names on the printed place cards until they'd finished the required events and were free to party. Several others joined them including Moose, Lance, Sara and Beth.

Everyone except Keenan was in a festive mood. He was quiet, more distracted than she'd ever seen him. Maybe he was nervous about the toast, though it was hard to believe considering his level of self-confidence.

A few minutes later, the band started playing and the bandleader called for Mr. and Mrs. Bart Gordon to take the dance floor. Thinking of Addison as Mrs. Gordon would take a while.

Appetizers continued to be served by traveling waiters.

Keenan excused himself to make a phone call.

It was a good half hour before he rejoined her. He was distracted and withdrawn from the conversation as if he'd left the wedding reception behind and moved into a private world.

She was determined not to ask about the call. If he wanted her to know, he'd tell her. He'd said there was no one waiting for him back home, but a man like him must have a lot of women after him.

Keenan remained that way the rest of the evening—not exactly ignoring her, physically close but emotionally distant. Josette decided it was likely the kiss that had put him on edge.

Hours later as the guests began to trickle away, Josette stepped out on the now-empty fourth-floor terrace. Leaning against the metal railing, she watched the silver reflections of the moon on the Mississippi River.

Josette heard footsteps behind her. Without turning, she knew it was Keenan who had joined her. He put his arms around her and spooned her body against his.

"At the risk of being redundant, did I tell you that you are breathtakingly gorgeous tonight?" he whispered.

"No, I don't believe you mentioned that."

"The second I saw you take one step down the aisle, you literally took my breath away."

She turned in his arms. "Really? Because I'm getting the distinct impression that you're growing bored with me and my multitude of life complications. Not that I blame you."

"Where did you get an idea like that?"

"You've been preoccupied much of the evening. I assumed you were regretting last night's kiss."

"Regret? Hardly. I dreamed about that kiss half the night."

"Then what's wrong? And don't tell me nothing, because I won't believe you."

He ducked his head, then met her eyes. "I was trying not to ruin your entire evening, but I can see I may as well be straight with you."

"Please do."

"Detective Hyde called me tonight. There's a new development in his investigation. He thought it best you hear about it from me before you heard it anywhere else."

"Just say it, Keenan. I'm not a child who needs protecting. I can handle the truth."

From the way he looked at her, she was suddenly not so sure.

Chapter Fourteen

Keenan knew of no easy way to sugarcoat this. He'd never been good at that anyway and there was no point in lying to Josette. She'd see through it in a second.

"A few hours ago a female body was pulled out of Bayou Lafourche about ten miles south of your dad's house."

Josette wrapped her arms tight around her chest and stared out at the Mississippi River for what seemed like an eternity before turning back to face Keenan. "What does this have to do with me?"

Her voice was so soft he could barely hear her, strain affecting her every syllable.

"Detective Hyde believes there's a chance the body could be your mother."

He felt her tremble, though she kept up a brave front. "Why would he think that? He wouldn't just call me to come look at a body if he had no solid clue to lead him to Isadora. He must have told you something more."

"He claims he only wants to rule out that possibility quickly before the media run with it."

"How long has the body been in the water?"

"They can't say until they get a more accurate forensics report, but one of the cops on the scene thinks no more than a week."

Josette took a deep breath and exhaled slowly. "Then it can't be Mother. She hasn't been in this area for over a year. If she were, she would have let me know."

Keenan wished he was as sure of that as Josette was. From the little he'd learned about Isadora, he didn't put anything past her. And no one seemed to understand her weird bond with Antoine, who was behaving strangely himself.

"What else?" Josette asked. "I want to hear it all now, not have it measured out like foul-tasting medicine."

"Detective Hyde said he got a tip by phone yesterday that danger was coming to Alligator Cove and that only Antoine Guillory could stop it."

Keenan had been dreading having to tell Josette that ever since he'd heard the words from the detective. He was amazed that Josette stayed as calm as she did, though it was killing him knowing how much this was hurting her and how much more it would hurt if the body turned out to be Isadora.

"Exactly when did you and Detective Hyde have this lengthy conversation?" she asked him.

"He left me a message when we were walking from the cathedral to the reception. I called him back during the reception."

"Why didn't you tell me then?"

"You were here to celebrate the wedding of your best friend. I thought you deserved at least a few hours without being hit by another bombshell. Besides, they don't know how long it will be before they move the body from the crime scene to the morgue. You could have ended up waiting hours at either location."

"Call Detective Hyde and tell him I want to see the body as soon as possible, wherever it is." She stiffened and stepped away. "Never mind. I'll call him myself."

A few minutes ago, she'd been trembling. Now she was taking charge and giving orders. She wasn't only smart, beautiful and talented, she had spunk. The bad thing about spunk was that in the wrong situation, it could be dangerous.

Isadora Guillory tended to keep life interesting and mysterious. She might have become involved in almost anything, could have easily shown up back in Alligator Cove or anywhere else in the world.

All Keenan was certain of was that he planned to make damn sure Josette's body didn't get pulled from an alligator-infested bayou. He was here to keep her safe, whether she wanted his help or not.

It was three in the morning when two detectives Josette hadn't met before led her and Keenan down a long, institutional gray hallway to a room at the far end of the morgue. Other investigators were still in the spot where the body had been found.

A continuing chant echoed in her mind. *Not my mother. Not my mother. Not my mother.*

Detective Hyde wasn't with them at the morgue. That had to be a good sign. If the detective had even the slightest belief the body could be Isadora Guillory, surely he'd be here to find out in person.

The deputy in charge stopped at a gray metal door and put his hand on the knob. "Are you ready, Ms. Guillory?"

She swallowed hard as Keenan put a hand to the small of her back and they stepped inside.

The body was laid out on a long, rectangular table. Josette pulled the bulky sweater she was wearing tight around her and shoved her hands into the front pockets of her favorite ripped jeans that she would never wear again.

She was immediately thankful for the menthol salve a deputy had given her to put under her nose in order to cut the sickening smell of human decay.

"This isn't going to be easy for you to look at," the deputy warned. "The body is exactly as it was when it was pulled from the bayou this afternoon, including bits of algae and other vegetation clinging to her skin. Forensics never wants to lose a scrap of evidence."

"I understand, but can we just get this over with for now?" Her heart felt as if it would pound out of her chest and she wanted only to flee from this room as fast as possible.

A crime scene expert stepped to the end of the table, took the corners of the pale gray sheet that had loosely covered the body and pulled it down until the body was on full display.

Josette went limp. She struggled to breathe. The

bones encased in the translucent, damaged skin that lay in front of her weren't a person at all. They were an empty vessel.

She'd never imagined that death was this potent. Fighting the urge to retch, she put a hand over her mouth and ran from the examination room to the ladies' bathroom they'd passed on the way down the hall.

Keenan followed her and held her head while she threw up in the toilet.

When she had nothing left in her stomach, he dampened a paper towel from the dispenser and handed it to her.

She pressed it against her forehead until her insides calmed a bit.

"It's not my mother," she said.

"Are you sure?"

"I'm sure. Did you see a heart tattooed on the victim's forearm? No. My mother had one right here." She touched the underside of her wrist. "I remember because tattoos are not allowed for the character she plays on *The Winds of Scandal*. She always complained that the makeup artist had to cover it up."

There was another reason as well, one Josette would keep to herself for now. Even dead, her heart would have recognized her mother.

Yet, staring at the cold void of what had once been a living, breathing human being was a harsh new reality for Josette. She'd convinced herself for a year that her mother could not be dead.

Isadora was simply off on a search for herself as she had done before. Perhaps she'd been successful this time and she wasn't ready to come back to her old lifestyle.

At worst, she might be hurt, or sick, but not dead. A woman as vibrantly alive as Isadora had always been couldn't possibly be dead.

Death was real. Death was final. Death was invincible. But not Isadora.

DAWN WAS ALREADY flirting with the horizon when the keys to Brad's BMW were apparently handed to the one person on duty to handle early morning valet service at the hotel.

Keenan realized more than ever what a good friend Bart was even though they seldom saw each other.

Addison's family had been just as accommodating, insisting the Princess Suite be extended for two more days, on their tab.

The newlyweds hadn't returned last night. Instead, they'd checked into a hotel near the airport for an early morning flight to Venice. That left Keenan with a room of his own and Josette with a luxurious two-bedroom suite.

Deciding on who slept where would have been a far more interesting dilemma if both he and Josette weren't both too drained of energy to finish what they'd started the night before.

They took the elevator to the second floor and walked to the suite in an eerily silent hotel. Thankfully, the paparazzi seemed to be under control for now. Josette slipped her magnetic key into the slot, opened the door and stepped inside the room.

She pushed her hair back behind both ears and shivered as she crossed her hands over her chest.

"I know it sounds weird, but suddenly this beautiful suite feels hauntingly empty without Addison. I dread the thought of staying in here alone for what's left of the night."

Keenan wasn't sure he'd heard her right. She was practically falling asleep standing up. So was he. Yet if he were to lie down beside her... Best not to even go there in his mind.

"The suite has two bedrooms. I'll keep my own and you could take the master one where Addison slept if that's okay," Josette said. "I mean if it's not too much of an imposition."

"It's no imposition at all if you're sure it's what you want."

She nodded. "I'm sure."

"In that case, I'll grab a few things from my room and be right back."

"Take your time," she said. "I need a long, hot shower myself, though I know soap and water can't wash tonight's gory images from my mind."

Josette turned and disappeared through her bedroom door.

A hotel suite fit for royalty, the most gorgeous and seductive woman that Keenan had ever spent a night with, or what little was left of this night, and he'd be sleeping by himself. The guys in the Bureau would love this.

He checked the sliding doors to the balcony before

leaving. They were locked, with the light and noise reducing drapes closed. "All safe and secure."

In his room Keenan took care of business quickly, showered, brushed his teeth, pulled on a clean shirt and a pair of jeans. He packed a duffel and carried it with him.

He entered the Princess Suite with the key card she'd given him. The only illumination was the sliver of light that shone from beneath the door of Josette's room. He tapped lightly, not wanting to wake her if she'd fallen asleep but also not wanting to chance startling her.

No response. He eased her door open. Her bed was empty, the sheets turned down and waiting. A panicky rush of adrenaline raced through him in the brief second before he spotted her curled up in a comfortable chair near the window.

Her eyes were closed, her wet hair dripping onto the top of a satiny blue sleep shirt. Her pert breasts were outlined beneath the damp, clingy fabric. Her bare legs dangled over one arm of the chair.

He lifted her into his arms and carried her to bed. A raw, sensual urge tore through him without warning. He ached to crawl between the sheets with her and fall asleep with her in his arms.

His body burned with desire despite the fatigue, but this was not the time nor place to lose control. He tucked her between the sheets before the need for her drove him completely over the edge.

He stepped into the other bedroom but left both

their doors open a crack so that he'd hear her if she needed him for anything at all.

How could he fight the attraction any longer? He'd never fallen this hard before.

Yet he couldn't imagine this could go anywhere after this weekend.

She was a beautiful, super talented designer from Nashville. Daughter of a multimillionaire, an heiress who'd one day afford yachts or mansions in the south of France.

Keenan was FBI and loved it.

How could they tackle the challenge of making that work?

Chapter Fifteen

Keenan jerked awake to the sound of loud voices coming from the street below. It only took a moment for him to realize where he was and why he was there.

The emotional visit to the morgue. The sensual blow he'd felt when carrying Josette to the bed and tucking her beneath the luxurious sheets. The way his life was changing with every heartbeat.

Keenan had already abandoned the simple rule that had been drilled into him since his first FBI undercover assignment. No romantic entanglements with a possible suspect or someone you're protecting.

Josette wasn't a suspect and technically she shouldn't need to be protected. But the neighborly little bayou community where her dad had lived all his life seemed to suddenly harbor a multitude of dangerous secrets.

He kicked off the sheets and threw his legs over the side of the bed just as his phone began to vibrate. He grabbed it quickly. The caller ID said Antoine Guillory.

For a second, he thought he'd picked up the wrong phone. But no, Antoine was calling him.

Keenan made his way to the balcony, managing not to yelp when his big toe bumped against the metal frame. His hello became a painful groan when he reached the balcony.

"Did I wake you?" Antoine asked.

"No," Keenan said. "Have you talked to Detective Hyde?"

"I'd like to talk to you first."

That was a surprise, unless Antoine wanted to warn him again to stay away from his daughter. "What can I help you with?" Keenan asked.

"Before we talk, I need to tell you one thing. I'd prefer Josette not know about this conversation until I know better how to handle this."

"Keeping secrets from Josette is not easy," Keenan said. "I'm sure you know that."

"At any rate, I don't know if you're the best person for me to talk to, but I know Josette solidly believes in you and that goes a long way with me. Where is my daughter now?"

"Josette and I are both still in the hotel in the French Quarter. I'm on the balcony right now trying to keep from waking her. She's asleep in the suite she shared with Addison, but I expect her to stir any moment now."

"I'm sure the first thing she'll want to do once she hears the morning news is to head to Alligator Cove."

"I assume you mean the news about the body being

taken from the bayou. If so, I can assure you that Josette saw the body and it isn't Isadora."

"Good. Then I guess we can meet at my house."

"If you're sure that's what you want," Keenan told him.

"I'm not sure of anything, but we have to do something, and we can't put it off any longer."

"What do you want to talk to me about?"

"A kidnapping."

"Whoa. Did I hear that right? Are you saying that you believe Isadora Guillory has been kidnapped?"

"All I'm sure of is that someone—maybe several someones—are demanding a ransom from me in order to free Isadora."

"Free her from whom? From where?"

"That wasn't made clear. Apparently, she's being held hostage but there was no clue as to where or why she is being held."

"How did this person or persons communicate his orders with you?"

"I got a note on Thursday, attached to my shrimp boat."

"Was it handwritten?"

"Yes, but—" Antoine hesitated. "Look, I know I messed up. I was so distraught, so angry that I balled it up and threw it in the bayou."

Keenan didn't have the heart to chastise the man for his stupidity. Instead, he asked, "What did it say?"

"The note specified that I must have twenty-four thousand dollars in cash ready for exchange sometime before midnight on Mardi Gras day. If there is any sign of a cop anywhere around, they will kill Isadora. And they warned they were deadly serious."

"KEENAN." JOSETTE'S VOICE was raspy. Even that increased his pulse rate.

"It's just me," he said. "Sorry for waking you."

"You didn't. I was already fighting my way out of the dregs of sleep."

She was still in bed, her ebony-colored hair haloed against the snowy white pillow. Her gaze locked with his, her dark, expressive eyes mesmerizing.

How could anyone look that good on so little sleep?

"What time is it?" Josette asked.

"A few minutes before ten."

She jerked up on her elbows. "Tell me you're kidding."

"Nope. You're sleeping through the excitement. The daiquiri shops will have a roaring business going by now."

"I can skip the daiquiri, but I'd kill for a coffee."

"Great idea," Keenan said. "You order. I'll brush my teeth, throw on some clothes and be right out."

His phone vibrated as he shut her bedroom door behind him. He checked the caller ID.

"Morning, Moose. What are you doing up before noon?"

"Sara just got a call from Beth who got a call from Mrs. Landry who got the news from an app on her phone. Bad news travels fast."

"If you're talking about the body the police pulled from Bayou Lafourche yesterday, the news could have been a lot worse for Josette. She viewed it in the morgue in the wee hours of the morning and determined it wasn't Isadora."

"That's not the story the press is peddling," Moose said.

"I'm sure their tale is far more tantalizing," Keenan said. Yet not nearly as fascinating and creative as the truth. He wondered how much of that Josette would have to deal with before this day was over.

"Did they mention Josette?" Keenan asked.

"Not that I heard. Are you and Josette still planning to visit her dad this afternoon?"

"Unless she's changed her mind overnight and I don't see that happening."

"Do you and Josette need us to go with you?" Moose offered.

"No, we're fine with just the two of us."

"I noticed."

A few minutes later, Josette joined him for coffee in the living room of the suite, fully dressed.

"Mind if I turn on the TV for a few minutes?" Josette asked.

"No, but I should warn you that you may not like what you see and hear."

"I'd be shocked if I did."

Josette channel surfed and landed on a local station that was interrupting its festival coverage with the breaking news.

"There is speculation that a body recovered from Bayou Lafourche yesterday could possibly be that of

television superstar Isadora Guillory, wife of local shrimper Antoine Guillory."

Josette jumped up, the coffee nearly spilling at the sudden movement. "Dad's right. This is far worse than simple harassment. The NOPD obviously released that information after I assured them that wasn't Mother."

"Do you want to call your dad?"

"No. Let's just hit the road." She put down her coffee cup, then headed out the door. "I'll text Dad along the way. He may refuse to talk to me, anyway."

To Josette's surprise, Antoine was not only willing to talk to her, he was waiting at the door when they arrived at his house. Coffee cup in hand, he waved them in. He looked far more worried than happy to see her, however.

"I don't know what's gotten into you, Dad, but it's nice to be invited into the house instead of being pushed away."

Antoine sipped his coffee. "You may change your mind when you hear what I have to say."

"Then we should go ahead and get it over with."

Antoine nodded in agreement. He led them inside and when everyone was seated, he wasted no time. "I've received a ransom demand for your mother. They're asking for twenty-four thousand dollars to be paid before the end of today."

Josette felt her heart crumble. "Someone has Mother? Who? Where? Is she safe? Have you talked to her?"

Antoine shook his head. "No one has talked to

me or gotten back to me since I received the note on Thursday."

"Where is the money?"

"I'm getting it together," Antoine said.

Getting it together? Was that why he sold the *Lady Isadora*? The timing was right. She remembered he'd said the sale would go through on Tuesday.

"Why didn't you tell me about the kidnapping, Dad? I was here but you said nothing." She added one more thought. "Why didn't you ask me for the money?" Secretly she railed inside at her father's stubbornness not to use his access to Isadora's fortune. Apparently, he was too stubborn to ask her for it, too.

Antoine dragged a hand through his hair. "I couldn't. The kidnappers said to tell no one. I had to follow their instructions—" His breath caught and his voice was tight when he spoke again. "All I want is Isadora back home again—at any cost."

"It's a little more complicated than that," Keenan said.

The grave tone of his voice sucked the last breath out of Josette.

ANTOINE COULD NO longer sit still. He bolted out of his seat and paced the room.

"It's not the money I'm concerned about," he insisted to Keenan. "It's a case of making the right move. Right now, we have no proof that Isadora is safe or that anyone can produce her. That's why I figured you could give me some guidance in how to handle all of this."

"I think you've made your first sound decision," Keenan said. "If you try to handle this without going through the cops, you will not only be breaking the law but putting Isadora and yourself in danger."

Josette jumped out of her chair and went to Antoine. "Where is Mother supposed to be now?" she asked.

"I don't have a clue. They make all the decisions. All I do is show up with the money when they say." He took off his hat and raked a hand through his hair. "I can't think straight. I'm worried that some kook found her and decided to make a fortune for himself."

"Only, of course, twenty-four thousand isn't a fortune," Keenan said. "Especially when you're talking about Isadora Guillory's kind of wealth. If you'd planned an abduction of someone that rich and famous, you'd be looking for big bucks. Close to a million or more. In my estimation, this isn't a ransom, it's an act of desperation."

"What do you mean, Keenan?" Antoine asked.

"I mean, it sounds like a distressed person who's in such dire need of cash that he's willing to kidnap Isadora...or pretend to."

Josette waved her hand to stop that line of thinking. "We have to assume whoever made the demands has her. I won't gamble with my mother's life and call the kidnapper's bluff."

Her eyes implored him for help. "The FBI was involved in the beginning of Mother's disappearance. Why can't they put you in charge now?"

"They have someone in charge," he explained. "But that doesn't mean I can't be here for you."

Her lips formed the words *Thank you* as Antoine ran into the kitchen. "I'm calling Detective Hyde now."

For a few minutes, Keenan had almost forgotten that Isadora was a lot more than Josette's mother. She was Antoine's wife, the woman he had always loved.

Keenan was only beginning to understand love and how it could steal your very soul.

Chapter Sixteen

Once Detective Hyde and two additional detectives arrived, they spent the next hour discussing methods utilized in kidnappings such as the one they were dealing with. Since Antoine had received the ransom demands and was supposed to receive the next instructions, he would stay at home with two lawmen.

Isadora Guillory was considered a very important subject. World-famous actress and multimillionaire. The crime was to be treated with the highest rank, significance and status.

Josette was to continue life as she knew it, lest the kidnapper get wind that Antoine had dragged her into it. Keenan was to keep an eye on Josette at all times. While not officially working for the police department, it was clear Max Hyde judged him to be totally competent.

Life as usual meant celebrating Mardi Gras by dining on crawfish at Cormier Shrimp and Crab Shack. Keenan figured mingling among the locals might yield some useful information, as well.

Tantalizing aromas met him the second he opened

his car door. So did the noise and zydeco music. He opened the passenger door for Josette and linked his arm with hers as they maneuvered their way through the crowded parking lot.

Another time, he'd have found this experience today fascinating. Now all he wanted to do was take Josette away from the angst that was devouring her. She was worried about her mother and her father, everyone except herself. Keenan was doing enough of that for both of them.

Problem was, worrying in the background wasn't his style. He yearned to be on the active side of this investigation.

He didn't understand the crush of uninhibited attraction that had exploded between them in five short days. All he knew was that what had started as harmless attraction had taken over his heart and mind.

Unless he was reading all the signals wrong, Josette was experiencing that same smoking chemistry. He wasn't sure if the situation they were dealing with caused the overwhelming magnetism or merely intensified it.

They stepped inside the low-slung wooden restaurant with the metal roof. The zydeco band was rocking the place so loud it seemed to vibrate the walls. The dance floor was jam-packed with people of all ages, keeping the beat and swinging their partners.

Others crowded around newspaper-covered tables, platters overflowing with boiled crawfish and crabs getting all their attention. Shells were heaped into mountainous piles in the middle of the tables.

In between all of that were rolls of paper towels, bottles of hot sauce and pitchers of cold beer.

Several people waved and called to Josette. He marveled how she kept a smile pasted on and waved back under the circumstances. He knew her insides were so tight she was near to cracking.

"Who's the bearded guy at the bar staring me down?" Keenan asked.

"That's T-Jack, Lorraine's uncle who owned all this land and the restaurant in the past. He also used to own and operate an extremely successful chain of seafood markets throughout South Louisiana."

"*Used* to own?"

"He had a heart attack a couple of years back. Lorraine claims his health problems forced him to sell the business, but unofficial word is that he double-crossed the wrong men and ended up going bankrupt. Somehow Lorraine took over the business but according to Dad, it's been rough."

The comment wasn't lost on Keenan. Had Lorraine seen a way to make a quick payday?

"Let's take a walk out back," Josette said. "That's where they cook the crawfish. It's a real hands-on job."

She introduced Keenan to several other patrons on the way out. Fortunately, the restaurant was too noisy to get into conversations beyond hello and a mention of concern for her mother from those who'd caught the morning news or heard it on the grapevine.

The scene behind the restaurant was almost as lively as it had been inside. Several propane burners fired huge pots filled with crawfish, corn, red potatoes and spices so strong they burned Keenan's nostrils. A half dozen or so men handled the cooking chores. A dozen or so more stood around gabbing.

A few yards away, out of the path of the smoke, several foursomes of guys sat at folding card tables playing *bourré*. Keenan had learned the basics of the card game at college, though he'd never played well.

Other men stood around, talking and nursing beers. A cluster of women sat on chairs under a tree drinking iced tea and chatting.

One of the ladies walked over to join Josette. They hugged and Josette looked pleased to run into her.

"This is Noelle," Josette said, "a friend since kindergarten. And the only friend from Alligator Cove who visited me in New York."

"Every time you talked Isadora into sending me a plane ticket," Noelle said. "We had a blast, going to the theater and thriving on the Big Apple excitement. Always thought I might end up there, but here I am teaching high school on the bayou."

Noelle turned her gaze to Keenan and then turned back to Josette. "Who's your friend?" she asked.

Keenan introduced himself.

"Here for Mardi Gras?" Noelle asked.

"No, a friend's wedding," he said. "Both of us are, or rather were. The wedding was last night."

Noelle turned back to Josette. "I'm really glad you showed up here today. I heard the news this morning and I couldn't decide if I should call you or not. You must be terribly upset."

Josette told her the body that had been pulled from

the bayou was not her mother. "Feel free to share that bit of information with everyone. I'm starting to feel like I'm just fodder for the show's publicity."

"I will. Once your mother hears the crazy rumors about her being dead, I'm sure she'll get in touch with you or Antoine to assure you she's fine."

"I hope you're right about that. Every time my phone rings, I pray it's her."

"A lot of people around here, including the police, don't understand how your mother can disappear for months at a time and not get in touch with her family. I say those people have never had a mob of paparazzi in their face every time they step out the door. That would make me bonkers."

"Me, too," Josette agreed, "but at times Mother seems to thrive on the attention."

"I know your dad and mom are separated, but they always seem totally into each other when I've seen them together."

"When was the last time you saw them together?" Josette asked.

"A couple of weeks before she disappeared. Hubby and I ran into them at a neighborhood bar in Lafayette one night. They were laughing and dancing together like lovers. We didn't intrude."

"No papparazzi?" Keenan questioned.

"No. I don't think anyone recognized her. She was wearing a wig and no makeup, and I'm certain no one expected to see a celebrity of her stature there."

"Have you shared that information with the police?" Keenan asked her.

"I went to the local police as soon as I heard Isadora was missing and they sent Detective Hyde out to talk to me. He didn't seem to think it was important at the time, but he questioned me again in detail ten days ago. Frankly, I was pleasantly surprised he was still searching for Isadora."

So, Isadora had been here to visit her ex two weeks before she'd disappeared. That was news to Keenan and evidently to Josette, as well. Another kink in the frayed rope that held the mystery together.

Keenan knew anytime someone went missing for as long as Isadora had, the odds for their safe return were going down fast. For now, Keenan's top priority for every breath he took would be keeping Josette safe. He walked over to get a better view of the cooking and to give Josette a chance to visit with her friend.

As he walked away, his phone rang. Dwayne Evans. Something new must have turned up. Hopefully, it wouldn't be bad.

AFTER CHATTING WITH Noelle for a few more minutes, Josette was about to go look for Keenan when she noticed Lorraine's son Daniel had joined a group of guys near where the cooking was going on.

She walked over and stopped at his elbow. "Happy Mardi Gras, Daniel."

He jerked to attention and turned to face her. "Well, look who's graced us with her company." Sarcasm dripped from his words. "You're pretty much the last person I expected to see out here today."

"Really? My dad does still live here."

"Does he? I thought he might have moved on by now."

"You and my dad have always been great friends and working buddies. What's the problem?"

"You can thank Isadora and his blind loyalty to her for most of Antoine's problems. If she asked him to harness a team of alligators for her, he'd give it a shot."

Josette shook her head. "That's not fair. My parents didn't make it as a couple, but they've remained friends. That's more than you can say for a lot of divorced people."

Daniel's eyebrows arched. "Friends? Face it, Josette. Your mother has strung Antoine along for years. She drops in once or twice a year, plays him for a fool and then walks out on him again. You know that better than anyone. Unfortunately, my mom's not smart enough to stay clear of the repercussions."

Josette couldn't totally deny any of that, but Daniel had never turned on Antoine before. He'd worked on the ship with Antoine since he was barely big enough to help cast a net.

According to her dad, Daniel knew as much about the shrimping business as anyone who fished the bayou.

Excluding Antoine, of course.

"I'd really like to know what happened between you and my father," Josette said.

Daniel shrugged his broad shoulders. "It's not much of a mystery. He up and decided to sell the

Lady Isadora to some stranger without giving me a chance at it."

"Did you tell him you were interested? Did you ask if you could work some kind of deal with him?"

"More than asked. I pleaded with him to sell me the boat. I just needed time to arrange a loan. He refused to give me any kind of break and we both know he could afford it."

Time. That was the one thing her dad didn't have. He needed the cash in hand by today. Maintaining a pretense, she told Daniel, "That doesn't sound like my dad. Maybe it was about more than money."

"I don't doubt that. He's in this big rush to clear out of Alligator Cove now. We all figure Isadora is behind that, just another of her stunts to keep Antoine from marrying my mother. Mom's too good for him, anyway."

"I hardly think Isadora has anything to do with it. Dad hasn't even heard from her in over a year."

"That you know of," Daniel scoffed.

The comment piqued Josette's interest. "What's that supposed to mean?"

He shook off the question. "Suffice to say there's plenty of folks around here who think she may have met with more than she can handle this time. Not that I ever had any reason to wish your mother trouble, but folks around here know how she's treated Antoine. They figure if she's dead, she had it coming to her."

The words felt like a spear puncturing Josette's heart. True, Isadora didn't have any close friends in

Alligator Cove, but as far as Josette knew she didn't have any enemies, either.

Except for Lorraine, and her dislike stemmed from jealousy.

"My mother is not dead," Josette insisted, for her benefit as much as Daniel's. "And as for Dad selling his boat so fast, I'm sure he has his reasons." Reasons she'd never reveal.

"I'm not blaming you, Josette. You're just another pawn in your mother's game. In the meantime, you'd best just head back to Nashville before you get dragged into the kind of trouble a lady like you can't handle."

"That sounds like a threat."

"Take it any way you want." He shoved his hands deep in his jean's pockets, then turned and walked away.

Chapter Seventeen

Keenan may not know much about the bayou, but when he met up with Josette and they finally sat down to eat, he managed to put away a few pounds of crawfish in less time than it took Josette to finish her beer.

When he finished and used half a roll of paper towels to clean his hands, they rolled their shells in the newspaper the waitress had brought them.

"Have you ever been on a legitimate swamp tour?" Josette asked.

"You mean other than the one I got a brief glimpse of behind your dad's place or the one I saw from the car every time I drove I-10 toward New Orleans out of Baton Rouge?"

"The view from a car doesn't count, nor does the sloshy area you can reach by foot behind Dad's inlet."

"Then I guess the answer to your question would be no." He eyed her suspiciously. "Why do I fear you're about to change that?"

She grinned. "You're getting to know me."

"These shoes aren't made for sloshing," he said as he held out a foot to the side of their table.

"You won't get too wet unless you fall out of the pirogue," Josette assured him.

"No guarantees there," he said, "but I'm game if you're brave enough to take your chances with me." He threw several bills on the table to cover their meals and a gratuity and stood, eager to get on with it. He knew Josette wasn't taking him on a sightseeing tour. There had to be a reason she was intent on getting on the bayou. "Are we going anywhere special?"

She cast a glance at the partiers within earshot, said nothing but gestured for him to follow. "We'll walk down to the nicer, more expensive cabins. That's where Lorraine keeps the wealthier guest pirogues. The rich prefer an upscale experience."

"Alligators included, I assume."

"Yes, but don't worry. I'll be certain you don't become gator bait."

"Can I get that in writing?"

"Sure. A waste of effort, though. You wouldn't be around to sue me if I didn't follow through. On the bright side, alligators are usually not aggressive unless you get too close to their babies, or they confuse you with food."

"Not particularly comforting. The giant mosquitoes out here think I'm rather tasty." He swatted one buzzing around his ear.

She took his hand as they started on a gravel path that snaked along a narrow inlet.

"Care to tell me now where we're headed?" he asked her. "Are we by any chance looking for kidnappers?"

She raised her brows as she looked at him. "Ya got me." She ducked under a low-hanging moss-laden bough. "You have to admit this would be the perfect place to hold a hostage. And since that hostage is my mother…"

"I'm right beside you." No way he'd leave her to investigate alone. Despite the alligators.

She stopped beside a cluster of cypress trees partially hiding several pirogues. Quickly she unlatched the combination lock of one of the small, flat-bottomed boats.

"How did you know the combination?" Keenan asked. "Or does Lorraine never change it?"

"She changes it monthly, but she has a pattern that apparently, she hasn't changed in years. Daniel and I used to sneak down here, get in a pirogue and play like we were pirates."

"Did you spend much time with him when you came to Alligator Cove?"

She nodded. "Right here on the bayou. He wasn't afraid of anything, so I had to pretend I wasn't, either."

"Is Daniel's dad still in the picture?"

"I'm not sure he ever was. I've never heard Daniel or anyone else mention him."

Josette casually leaned over and brushed a spider off her right sleeve. "Let's head out to some of the more rugged cabins."

"Are there fewer creatures crawling inside them?" he asked as he sidestepped the spider that was the size of a half dollar.

"You know, some people like a challenge," she teased him.

"Take my word for it. I'm a wimp."

"Right. A wimp who fights terrorists."

Keenan helped her lift the lightweight boat and carry it the few feet back to the muddy bank of the water. A couple of bullfrogs croaked loudly at the disturbance to their environment.

Two turtles sunning on a huge rock jumped into the water. No sign of snakes or gators, but something that looked like a huge rat with protruding orange teeth stared at them from the opposite bank.

"You grow your mice big down here."

"That's a nutria," Josette said, "sometimes called coypu or swamp rat by the locals."

"Not your normal rodent."

"They're not as bad as they look," Josette said. "Biggest problem with them is they do a lot of gnawing damage to the bank."

"Don't do a lot for beautifying the scenery, either," Keenan said.

There were two oars and one long, metal pole tucked inside the pirogue. Keenan helped Josette into the boat and climbed in after her, taking a seat and picking up an oar.

"Just hold on to the oar for now," Josette said. "I'll demonstrate the art of poling a pirogue down the bayou."

"Gotta love a woman who knows her way around a pole," he teased.

She threw back her shoulders in a proud stance. "I'm not without skills."

"So, I'm learning."

She kept standing and used the pole to push and guide them through a shallow spit of brownish water choked with algae.

After a few minutes of watching Josette's gorgeous, nimble body adopt a swaying rhythm, Keenan decided he should do more than just watch and lust after Josette.

"Let me try my hand at that," Keenan said.

"Sure." She traded places with him.

He took over the task until they reached slightly more navigable water.

"You catch on fast," Josette said.

"That's just so we can get out of this boat sooner."

He took his seat and exchanged the pole for an oar. She took the other and with two oars in sync, they moved faster. A crane stepped into the water, lifting one leg gracefully as he searched for his dinner.

Keenan looked up as they passed beneath the overhanging limbs of a cypress tree. He sucked in his breath as he spotted a long, black snake dangling from the bottom branch.

"Don't worry," Josette assured him. "That one's safe. The one swimming along the bank to your left isn't."

He turned and caught sight of a large cottonmouth moccasin a few feet from his oar. That one he knew could be deadly.

He was fast coming to the conclusion that this was not a good idea for a city boy like himself. But he'd tough it out for Josette's sake. And maybe her instincts would prove right.

The bayou split off again and she pointed to the shallower choice. That's when he spotted the snout of an alligator coming toward them. Another followed close behind. The gator swam right past them and kept going. Keenan managed to breathe again and wondered why anyone ever did this for fun.

"Adventurous or not, I can't imagine anyone pays to stay in that dilapidated pile of rust and warped wood, with gators for bodyguards," Keenan said, pointing to a ramshackle cabin that stood on stilts along the shore.

"They don't," she assured him. "I didn't know that one was still standing. Daniel and I only dared to explore that place once and that was only because of that makeshift bridge to the cabin."

"How old were you then?"

"Twelve. I was visiting Dad that summer and wanted to prove to Daniel I hadn't become a spoiled city brat."

"And did you?"

"Until he picked up a machete that was in the back of the cabin and started making up a story about a swamp monster who chopped people up. Then, worst of all, one of those giant flying cockroaches that are so infamous in the New Orleans area smacked me in the face and then fell into my hair. I think they heard my squealing all the way back to the French Quarter."

Keenan studied the decaying structure, imagining what creatures other than cockroaches might be slithering around inside it.

"Wait," Josette said, grabbing his arm. "I may have been wrong. Someone might be inside the cabin now."

"I don't see any movement," Keenan countered, his instincts on high alert.

"Maybe not, but there's a pirogue tied to that skinny cypress tree. It's got the crab shack's logo painted on it."

What would somebody be doing in a barely standing cabin? Could Josette be right? Could it be the kidnapper? If it was, she was far from safe, and he cursed his stupidity in allowing her to venture out here. Even worse, he realized, they could have stumbled onto the drug cartel.

"We should turn back and alert Hyde," he told her, but she was already leading the pirogue to shore. He knew nothing would stop her and now he was all that stood between her and potential danger.

THE WATCHER POCKETED the keys and exited the cabin, happy to leave the hairy creatures and scurrying insects behind and drag in a humid breath.

All was going according to plan. You could always count on people sticking their nose where it didn't belong. A chuckle escaped and a hand went up to stifle it. Shh. Don't want to be found just yet.

Tiptoeing deeper into the palmettos and cypress

trees would provide a good vantage point to watch the action. Or at least hear it.

No apologies here. No regrets. That's what they got for not minding their own business.

The watcher sat on a cypress root, legs splayed in front, ears tuned in.

Can't wait to hear their screams.

KEENAN HELD HER hand as they crossed the bridge and approached the cabin. He scanned the area, looking for any signs of life. Human or otherwise. Seeing none, he pushed on the slanted, metal door and it gave, nearly falling off the rusty hinges. That's all it took. The creatures magnified in abundance. A spider bigger than his hand fought its way through a door-size tangle of webs. Rats the size of large squirrels ran along the baseboards. Huge cockroaches, scorpions, ants and a vicious-looking tarantula all seemed to be daring them to fight them off.

He pushed Josette behind him and battled with the spiderwebs before entering.

Old baskets and a few lightweight chests were stacked in one corner. Faded blankets, ripped sheets and a sleeping bag that he was pretty sure had shared its bed with the roaches he was sick of.

But there were indications that people might have stayed there—recently, too.

Empty cookie cartons. Fast-food wrappings. Bags of chips that were opened and scattered around the room. Peanut butter smeared on loaded rattraps.

"Since we're here, let's make sure we don't have to make a return trip," Keenan said.

"Exactly how do we do that?"

"Strain a few muscles. Turn over whatever isn't clearly visible and check the contents of the chests and trunks."

She pointed toward the broken boards and gaping holes in the floor. "Did you forget you have a bad leg?"

"It's not bad, just injured."

"No joking, please." Her voice shook and for the first time he realized his intrepid investigator was afraid.

They searched quickly and found nothing but more detritus. Keenan convinced himself that if anyone had been there earlier, they were gone now.

Sticking to the perimeter of the front room to avoid the holes in the floor, Josette trudged ahead. She motioned to another door at the back of the cabin. "I'm going to look in there."

He turned to examine a smudged piece of paper he'd missed on the first pass when he heard the door creak open and slam shut. What he heard next was like a nightmare escaping into reality.

Josette's screams mixed with the unmistakable sounds of snapping teeth.

He narrowly missed a foot-size hole as he ran to her, stopping just in time to avoid falling into a pool of brackish water filled with not one, not two, but close to twelve large and very angry alligators.

Fear unlike he'd ever encountered on a deadly

mission overtook him, but somehow he assessed the scene as he'd been trained to do. The floorboards of the back room had totally decayed and the bayou waters rose to just a foot beyond the doorway.

"Keenan!" Josette's frantic voice reached him. "Don't move an inch or you'll fall in." She was splayed against the wall, her arms out to the sides, seeking purchase in the knots of the wood.

Before them, the huge gators splashed. Several others appeared as if from another world. They began to swish about wildly, snapping their powerful jaws as they neared Josette and Keenan.

Staying close to the wall, Keenan reached her. "Grab my hand," he ordered, thankful he did know a bit more about staying alive than he did most anything else. "I'm going to open the door and together we'll jump through it. Then I'll shut it on the gators and we run. Fast."

But when he reached his right hand behind him, feeling for the knob, it wouldn't turn. The door was locked from the outside.

The gators closed in, only a two-foot gap from the floor to the water separating Josette's and Keenan's feet from their razor-sharp teeth.

"Keenan, hurry. We've got to get out of here." She grabbed a nearby pirogue pole and began hitting the gators on their snout, her courage no doubt rising from an unknown well inside her.

He pulled out his weapon and he led her away from the door, then fired rapidly, four shots in quick succession, enough to destroy the lock. Scampering closer, he stopped only to ram his right foot on the snout of one eager gator that got too close to Josette. Then he pushed his shoulder against the door and, holding hands, they fell into the front room. He slammed the door closed with his foot.

They scrambled up. "Let's go. Run as fast as you can," he yelled to Josette.

They didn't stop till they crossed the bridge and made it to pirogue.

Josette fell into the hollowed-out boat and Keenan steered them away from the cabin of horrors. He knew what had just happened was not an accident. It was planned, but by whom?

Right now the only thing he wanted was to get Josette to safety. That was all he'd ever want. That was the only thing he was certain of.

THE SICKENING FEELING of fear stayed with Josette as they walked back to the restaurant after storing the pirogue. No matter how hard she tried, she couldn't forget how close they'd come to death. One misstep and either she or Keenan or both of them would have fallen into the vat of snapping gators. She shuddered as she imagined their lifeless bodies—at least what would be left of them after the alligators had their fill of them—floating down the bayou. Distorting as they bloated with water.

She remembered last night, staring into the empty eyes of the body Hyde had called her to ID. A woman

who was no longer breathing. Her stare was empty.
Her heart no longer beating. Would she and Keenan
have looked like that?

Would her mother look like that when they finally
found her?

"I hate seeing you like this," Keenan said, his gentle touch making her stop walking. "Is there anything
I can say or do to help?"

"I can't stop thinking about the body we viewed
last night. No matter who she is, I'm sure there are
family members grieving for her. They'll never see her
alive again. Someone will never hold her in their arms
again. She was once their everything. Now she's…
gone." Her voice hitched. "And after what just happened, that could have been us."

Keenan pulled her into his arms. "I know it's only
been less than a week, but I can't bear to think what it
would be like not having you, Josette. I pretty much
think of you from morning till night."

She leaned back, looking into his eyes, and saw
the honesty there, the affection. Her gaze, she knew,
reflected the emotion. She cupped his jaw with her
palm. "I feel the same way, Keenan. But—"

His kiss cut off what she was about to say.

She reveled in the pressure of his lips, the explora-
tion of his tongue, and leaned in, pressing her breasts
against him. In his arms, she forgot everything—the
gators, her missing mother, the mysterious kidnapper. Everything but how good Keenan made her feel
and how much she wanted him.

"What happens now?" The words were a breathy whisper against his lips.

"I'm not sure, except that I know it should happen in the Princess Suite. Uninterrupted. No phones. Toss the robes and give the silky negligée only a brief starring role before it goes flying across the room."

It was exactly what she wanted, too. "Say the word and I'm there and then we can add one more miracle to this day," Josette said.

"What's the other one?"

"Deep down, I have to believe that Mom is coming home today. We'll celebrate for days—you, me, her and my father. Then she'll invite all her fans in on the party."

"No wonder her fans are so loyal and love her so much."

"Yes, but that's just the love she spreads like icing on the cake. It's impossible not to love her in return. You'll love her, too, Keenan. I can't wait for you to meet her. Dear God, just let her be alive."

Tears spilled from Josette's eyes. Worry hung heavy in her voice. Keenan's heart constricted. Even if he'd tried, he couldn't escape the fact that at this minute, his whole life was tied to Josette in ways he couldn't fully grasp. His burning fear was that he was going to lose her.

Not lose her to her parents and their problems. Not lose her to the career she loved. Not lose her to his career that demanded so much of him.

He was afraid of losing her to life, to never being able to give her enough.

"The day is only half-over," he reminded her. "There's still time for a miracle or two."

He prayed she'd get that miracle. But he was FBI. He knew miracles didn't always happen.

Chapter Eighteen

The day dragged on and on and on, with no word from her father or Detective Hyde. She yearned to call her dad and find out if he'd heard from the kidnapper, if he had received the ransom directions. But she knew she couldn't.

Images of her dead mother played in her mind on a loop, Isadora's face replacing that of the body she'd been called to identify. In her heart she couldn't believe that her mother could be dead, yet the cold, hard possibility that had been planted in her mind at the sight of the body last night continued to haunt her soul.

The only thing holding her together was that there was still protective, loving, exciting Keenan whose kiss literally drove her out of her mind. She could no longer fight the fact that she was falling in love with him, but it was accompanied by the reality that he'd be leaving soon. When she'd tried to tell him her fears earlier, he'd kissed her. But he'd made no mention of seeing her once they left New Orleans.

Smart, on his part. Even if he felt the same way

about her, that she did about him, they not only lived in different worlds, but on a different planet, or so it seemed.

His world depended on keeping innocent victims alive and keeping secrets.

Hers focused on designing ball gowns and fabulous outfits that made beautiful women look even more stunning.

At least, she pictured their careers conflicting that way. The scary part was that she couldn't picture any life without him in it. Nor did she want to picture any life where she could be happy without him in it.

Which defined her dilemma as much as anything could.

She couldn't figure it out with all that was going on now, but there had to be a way to fuse their lives.

"Should we head back to the hotel?" she asked.

"How do you feel about talking to Lorraine before we leave?"

"Any particular reason why I would? I'm not her best friend, by far," Josette said.

"I'm not sure any of the Guillorys are at this point. But she hears an awful lot of gossip talking to people at the restaurant every day. There's a chance she knows who's been out at that cabin."

Josette nodded. "She might even overhear about someone who's in such a dire need of money that they might consider abduction for a ransom."

"Or pretend to," Keenan corrected.

He took her hand and she walked beside him. Her

concerns about a future with Keenan would come later. Right now, she was more concerned about her future with Isadora.

IT TOOK THEM a little over half an hour to locate Lorraine. She was sitting at a folding card table behind the restaurant with a group of volunteer cooks and revelers who'd been there most of the day.

She looked tired, wiped out from her hosting duties.

"The party's still going, I see," Keenan said as they approached her.

Lorraine looked up, her eyes narrowing as she saw Josette and him. Clearly, she was none too pleased to see them again. "Mardi Gras is always a party, but tradition mandates that the Mardi Gras celebration ends no later than midnight before Ash Wednesday and the beginning of Lent."

"There are always a few guests here who make that a serious challenge," Daniel said, as he quickly walked over to them, a beer in hand. "I've been swept out with the night's trash in more French Quarter bars than I care to admit."

Lorraine took a deep breath and exhaled slowly. "Thankfully, most of my partiers don't push the limits that far, but I keep the restaurant and bar open for those who do."

Lorraine frowned up at Daniel. "Any more of those parties you need to confess?"

"No, Mom. I'm good. Just a handy cabin dweller on festival night now."

"And that's what you have the cabins for," Josette said. "Speaking of the cabins, it looked like someone might have been hanging around that old ramshackle cabin that looks unlivable, the one with the splintered bridge."

"That cabin is off-limits now and for good reasons," Lorraine said. "It has a no-trespassing sign on it now, or at least it did."

"Didn't notice one today," Keenan said.

"Did you and Josette go inside?" The irritation in Lorraine's voice was clear.

"Believe me, we weren't in there for long," Josette said. "Every kind of spider or gross creature on the bayou is in there."

"And yet you went in there?" Daniel questioned. Keenan couldn't tell if it was agitation or fear that held prominence in his tone.

"Let it go," Lorraine told her son. "Nobody was hurt this time and I'm guessing they found whatever they were looking for or they'd still be there."

"We weren't looking for anything specific," Josette said. "Just reliving my childhood adventurous days with Daniel." Keenan admired how she deflected the innuendo in Lorraine's comment. The woman was cagier than he thought. "I think I got out of there even faster today than I did last time."

Daniel laughed but the amusement didn't reach

his eyes. "Bloody machete man still out there waiting on you?"

The look on Lorraine's face reiterated that she didn't appreciate Daniel's humor today.

"Did either of you see Antoine today?" Keenan asked, deliberately changing the subject.

It was Daniel who answered. "No. Antoine has his own schedule these days. He's too busy getting rid of me and his shrimp boat, so he can go searching for his new life and his old wife."

Josette bristled. "Why are you turning on him or is that just the beer talking?"

Lorraine stood up from the table, confronting Josette. "Let's keep this straight without the fantasy ideas Isadora dishes out on *The Winds of Scandal.* Can't blame anyone but myself for letting it happen, but Antoine uses me the way Isadora uses him. She comes in and out of Antoine's life on an as-needed basis. He hasn't even heard from her in over a year. Nonetheless, if she walked up now after a year of abandonment, he'd welcome her back with open arms and not a question asked."

"She's his wife. He stands by her," Josette argued. "She may get her priorities mixed up from time to time, but their bond is still strong. You have no idea what my mother goes through in her professional life. You don't know the real Isadora."

"Apparently, no one does," Daniel said. "We can't all be superstars. Of course, some of us are better than others about keeping their promises. Isadora could probably teach you a thing or two about that."

Keenan could see the heat rise in Josette's cheeks and stepped in. He couldn't blame her. There was obviously no love lost between the Cormiers and Isadora. But was their hatred for her enough to harm her?

"Enough talk of Isadora from you and everybody else who's partied so much this afternoon," he said. "We should all be praying she does show up and that she's safe and healthy."

"Of course, we're concerned about her," Lorraine said, backing down. "It's just that she's done this so often before, she's made a game of it. We're praying we'll all be celebrating a reunion with her next week if not sooner."

Keenan sensed no sincerity in her voice and from the look on Josette's face, she didn't, either.

The party broke up on that note, and he knew Josette had to feel sick at heart about the way they'd been bad-mouthing her mother. He ushered Josette away and led her toward the car.

"Do you think we should go and take another look at that cabin?" Josette asked when she stopped at the passenger door.

Keenan shook his head. "I've seen enough. Let's go home or to the closest thing to it today."

Her face took on a wistful look. "For me, home would be Dad's place, though it's been a long time since I've actually lived there."

"Same here," Keenan said. "The day after I graduated, I left home and moved into the cheapest apartment I could find, my freezer supplemented with the best steaks from Dad's ranch and my sweet tooth satisfied with peach cobbler using the fruit from my mother's orchard."

"And from there you made the natural jump to counterterrorism?"

"I made a few sidesteps along the way."

"Such as?"

"Worked as a high-school football coach for one year. Thought I knew everything there was to know about the game of football. Found out really quick I didn't know anything about high school boys.

"We lost every game. I hated the boos. They must have, too, because they fired me."

"Was it time to go back home then?"

"Nope. I decided I was too tough for mere boys so I was on the verge of becoming a full-fledged marine, but the travel arrangements left a lot to be desired. Finally, met a very smart woman who sold me on the FBI. Her supervisor put in a good word for me. They hired me, and…"

"And the rest is history," Josette finished for him.

"No way. The beginning didn't even get started until I caught a plane to New Orleans one Friday afternoon on my way to a wedding and I met the most gorgeous woman that ever brushed me off."

Josette reached out to grab his hand and brought it up to her lips. She smiled as she kissed it. "But she was impressed by the effort," she said sincerely.

"Where is that very smart woman who led you into the FBI now?"

"At her house taking care of three kids and two dogs. She was a great partner, but just in case you're wondering, she was never anything more than a partner."

"I wondered. I didn't ask. I know you must have had a few women along the way."

"More than a few, but I never met anyone who affects me as you do." He leaned in, pressing her against the car, and wrapped his hands around her waist. When he dipped his head and touched his lips to her neck, she sighed. "I want to make love to you, Josette. I want it more than anything."

His lips were a breath away from hers when her phone rang. Her tongue swept across her mouth, leaving a wet trail that he longed to discover, but he knew she couldn't let the call go unanswered. Not now.

"It's Detective Hyde," she said when she looked down at the screen. After a few moments, she filled him on what the lawman had to say. "There's been no communication. No change in assignments, either. The two kidnapping experts are changing shifts now. But Hyde suggests we drive back to Antoine's. Hyde's meeting us there."

"Why the change in plans?"

She shook her head. "I'm not sure. All he said was Dad is getting increasingly nervous, and Hyde doesn't want to risk him making a dangerous move, whatever that would be at this point." Her brows knitted and her eyes looked troubled. He knew how difficult this had to be for her and he reached out for her hand.

She glanced down at their clasped hands. "Thanks."

"You're welcome, but for what?"

"For helping me make it through this nightmare."

He wanted to thank her, too. For making it so easy to love her.

But that had to wait. They had a kidnapping to solve.

Chapter Nineteen

Keenan slowed and killed the engine in the parking area in front of Antoine's house. "Looks like your dad has company."

Two men were walking the deck of the shrimp boat. Two other men appeared from the hull. None seemed interested in her or Keenan.

Josette's temper exploded. She'd taken about as much of this as she could stand. She jumped from the car and raced toward the ship. Keenan quickly caught up with her. She wasn't sure if it was to protect her or the men.

"That ship is private property," Josette called.

A blond, lean, tanned man wearing a fishing hat turned toward her. "We know," he called back. "We just bought it, or rather our boss did."

"I suppose you have proof of that sale."

"As a matter of fact, I do, but what makes it your business?"

"I'm Antoine Guillory's daughter."

"Your name's not on the deed but join us on the deck and you can check out the paperwork. It's all legal. Nothing for us to hide."

The man doing the talking seemed friendly enough, no sign of stress in his appearance or voice. Apparently, bearing the name of Guillory meant nothing to him, either.

Josette and Keenan approached the man on the deck. He handed Keenan a folder full of paperwork. Josette read over his shoulder as he checked it out.

She grew more anxious with each detail. The sale looked legit. The selling price was the shocker. Compared with prices Antoine had told her others paid for boats much smaller and less fancy than this one, Antoine had gotten about half of the boat's worth—maybe less.

Why hadn't her dad come to her? She would have given him the ransom money and he never would have had to practically give away the boat.

The man who'd done the talking reached for his pile of paperwork. "We'll be leaving and taking the shrimp boat with us."

"You stole this boat at this price," she protested. "My dad loves this boat."

"Reckon he needed the money more than he needed the boat." The men pocketed the paperwork and started up the engine.

They had no idea how right they were, Josette thought. Antoine needed the money and he'd had only days to get the ransom together, so he'd jumped into action and did what he thought would be the best move. He sold the shrimp boat and who knew what else.

That was the real heartbreaker. He would have

done anything to save Isadora if he believed she was in danger from crazy abductors. But, dear God, Josette prayed, don't let her be in danger now.

From now on, Josette would have to make sure her father at least kept some extra emergency money on him. Josette knew for a fact that Isadora had tried many times to get Antoine to take a monthly alimony check or whatever he'd prefer to call it. He'd always refused, his pride not letting him take money from his multimillionaire wife. As much money as Isadora donated to dozens of charities, she wouldn't have hesitated to write a check for whatever amount Antoine needed. Only this time, she couldn't. And now, Antoine was doing everything he could to protect her and Josette, the two women he loved most in this world.

Josette started toward the house. Her feet felt as heavy as bricks as she trudged up the steps. The minute she and Keenan went inside, she knew the heaviness all around them was about more than Antoine being nervous.

"What's going on?" Josette demanded as she ran to her father. "It's the kidnappers, isn't it? Did you talk to them?"

His shoulders slumped, Antoine nodded. "We talked but I'm not sure how much they heard. They said what they had to say and hung up."

"Did you tell them you have the ransom money?" Josette asked, her voice trembling.

Antoine only nodded.

Detective Hyde ushered her into a chair at the

kitchen table and sat down. "Unfortunately, we can't be sure of anything right now," he told her. "Mostly we don't know if the people demanding ransom are actually holding Isadora. They're for sure not the only people trying to cash in on *The Winds of Scandal*/ Jill Hawthorne viral rumor. However, much of that has died down now that Mardi Gras is approaching an end."

Antoine walked over and put his hand on his daughter's shoulder.

"We've got a great team working on this, Boo. They'll figure it out."

"I asked you before—did you tell them we have the money? When they call back, tell them we'll give them double what they asked for. I'll bring the cash to them in person if they'll just release Mother."

Keenan sat beside her at the table and took her hand. His fingers brushed over hers in a comforting gesture. "Like the detective said, so far, we only have their word that they have Isadora."

Max Hyde stood up. "From now on, no one leaves the house alone. If you go farther away than the front steps, let someone know. I think we can agree on that at this point, right?"

Keenan nodded. "Right there with you. If they do have Isadora or any record of contact with her, now would be the smart time to flaunt it. Otherwise, they're just any John Doe in the alley looking for some fool to hand over some cash."

"You make it sound as if you have a deck stacked with aces," Josette said.

"Just trying to use every trick in my box," Max said. "I'm in Homicide now, remember? Just so you know, all that time you complain that I spend investigating those unsolved crimes like Isadora Guillory, I'm doing the required legwork for success, not just driving down here to pick up fresh shrimp for dinner."

"What *do* we know, Detective?" Josette asked. "I mean know, not guess."

"Their recent phone call lasted less than thirty seconds. We copied down every word. They want twenty-four thousand dollars in unmarked bills. From the time of their next phone call, we should be able to reach the exchange point in fifteen minutes. Antoine must be alone. Any sign of a cop and they say they'll kill her. Her life and safety depend on us."

Keenan looked to Antoine. "Did you recognize the voice?"

He shook his head. "It was distorted. No, more like muffled, as if whoever it was was speaking through something over their mouth."

Detective Hyde looked at Keenan. "What do you read into the fifteen-minute exchange point?"

"I figure it's their way of making sure the money is in Antoine's hands when they call so that they'll have instant access once they set up the exchange. Otherwise, we'd have trouble even getting the money into the car on time much less to an exchange point that we'd have to drive to."

The men sat back down, gathered around the comfortable old table as if it was just a regular evening meal, yet the tension ran deep as they poured more coffee and analyzed over and over again what they thought would be the kidnapper's next move—if they had one.

"Is there any problem with my sitting on the front porch?" Josette asked.

"Not at all."

"Do you mind if I sit with you?" Antoine asked.

"I'd like that."

Neither talked for fifteen minutes or so, the same length of time the abductors were giving them to get from this porch to Isadora. Antoine didn't mention that, but Josette was certain he'd thought about it, too.

"I'm so sorry it's come to this, Josette," he said, finally breaking the silence. "I'm heartsick I didn't go with Isadora or persuade her to come home with me that last night I saw her."

"Don't blame any of this on yourself, Dad. When Mother makes up her mind to do something, there is no stopping her. Everyone knows that, especially me. She invited me to come to New Orleans with her that trip, too, but I had a work deadline. Besides, I'd gone with her before on shorter publicity trips. She has a way of forgetting you're there the moment the paparazzi and fans discover her."

"I know, but this time was different. I knew it but I was so afraid of having my heart broken again. Well, now it may be broken for good."

Hearing the agony in her father's voice, she took his hand. "What makes you feel so strongly that something was different this time?"

"She asked me to go away with her. Not in the

usual way, but as if she really needed me. At the last minute, I drove into town, needing to see her one more time before she left. When I got to the hotel, her fans were crowded all around her." He paused and brushed the sleeve of his shirt across his nose.

"I had come prepared to change my mind and go with her but then I backed down, sure she could never love just me."

"Do you love her, Dad?"

"I do. I finally realize how much. I spent too much time in the past worrying that I could never compete with what stardom could give her. I was hung up on holding to my roots instead of letting her feel free to go as far as she could in developing hers." He shook his head, regret dripping from the motion. "If I could get just one more chance, I'd do it differently. I'd find a way to make us work somewhere between New York and New Orleans." He turned to Josette and his sad eyes met hers. "If you ever find real love, Josette, don't ever let it go."

"I won't, Dad." It was excellent advice, she knew. Little did her father know she'd already found the love of her life. But could she find a way to not let Keenan go?

They sat in silence for a while as the skies turned a hazy gray. Just as she got up to go back inside, Lorraine's truck drove up. Leaving Antoine to deal with the unwanted and likely uninvited guest, Josette decided it was time for her to find out exactly where the ransom was being held and by whom.

Keenan was in the family room just off the kitchen,

sitting on the leather sofa, his left leg propped up on throw pillows, his cell phone to his ear, when Josette went back inside. Not wanting to disturb him, she walked down the hall to Antoine's bedroom, even though she knew she'd just left him on the porch with Lorraine.

The door was locked. Strange, since she couldn't remember the last time she'd known it to be locked. Perhaps that answered one of her own questions for her. That could well be the location of the ransom money.

Still curious, Josette walked down to the spare bedroom she used for rare overnight stays. It wasn't locked and the blue duffel bag that had been in Antoine's room was now here, lying on the top of the bed.

Josette unzipped the duffel. As before, it held the same folded, casual clothes and toiletries bag. Everything for a man ready to travel, a man destined to find his wife. At least that's the way she chose to take it.

As she pawed through the items, she saw something shiny at the very bottom. She remembered the first time she'd seen the duffel, how she'd seen something glimmer in the duffel but she hadn't had time to see what it was. Her father had been calling her and she didn't want to get caught rifling through his stuff.

Now she pulled it out and her breath caught. The glimmering object was the silky, sequined sapphire fabric of the dress her mother had worn on her last night in the French Quarter. The gown she'd worn to the Mardi Gras ball. The last night she had been seen.

Over the years, Josette had created several stunning outfits for Isadora to wear for special occasions. Without fail, Isadora raved about the cocktail dresses, but this had been the first one she'd ever worn for a truly special occasion.

It ended up being seen all over the world as the mystery of Isadora's disappearance became global news.

How had it ended up in her father's luggage?

Josette held it up to her, running her hands over the shimmering fabric. Finally she turned for a look in the full-length mirror. Horror glared back at her.

Harley Broussard smiled at her, his fingers wrapped around the trigger of a black revolver.

"Nice dress, Josette."

Chapter Twenty

Josette watched Harley Broussard close and lock the bedroom door behind him. Her instincts pressured her to scream, but she knew that would send Keenan rushing to her aid. Harley would be waiting on him, revolver in hand and ready to fire.

Her heart threatened to pound out of her chest, her mouth went dry, her throat tightened. Forcing in a breath, she said, "What are you doing here, Harley? What do you want?"

"You know what I want. Twenty-four thousand dollars. I'll need it in cash as requested, and I'll need it tonight if you want to live to see the sun rise in the morning. After that, neither you nor any of your rich friends and TV star family will ever have to see or speak to me again."

"No, because you'll be in prison," she spat out. She marveled at her own bravado, though inside she felt as if she were falling apart.

"You're wasting your time if you think you can frighten me off with that worthless, limping FBI agent you've got following you around like a puppy, pretending to be your protector. This will go much better for you if you keep Keenan and Antoine out of this. I know how you hate it when something or someone has to die."

He flashed his revolver, treating it like a toy, and then pulled out a second gun from a holster at his ankle.

At the mention of Keenan and her father, she tried to pull herself together. Right now, she was all that stood between them and this crazed gunman. "How did you get in here?" Josette demanded. She had to keep him talking while she frantically planned her next move.

"Not that it matters, but your father's girlfriend Lorraine drove me over. Antoine opened the door for me while your boyfriend was on the couch absorbed in a phone call. See what good that bodyguard has done for you?"

The bile in her stomach felt as if it were beginning to boil. "This was never a kidnapping or an abduction. You don't have Isadora. You never did. You're nothing but lies, lies, lies."

It had never been about the money to Josette. It was Isadora who she feared for, the one who mattered. And now she realized that there was no plan for a ransom and no chance that Harley had Isadora. And no chance her mother would be coming home tonight. But Isadora was alive. Josette refused to believe anything else, no matter how many of her mother's dresses Harley produced.

"How did you get her dress?" She may not make it out of this room alive, but she had to know.

"Easy enough," he replied willingly. From the glimmer in his eyes, he was proud of himself. "I stole it from her hotel room."

She remembered him saying he was working at the hotel at the time of her mother's disappearance. "Why was it in my father's duffel?"

"The better to frame him with."

His smugness made her stomach roil. "What makes you believe anyone would—"

The glimmer disappeared and Harley's face twisted into a visage of pure evil. "Enough! Get the money. *Now.*" He started to shake with rage. "Either I leave here with the money tonight or I die. And if I die, I won't be going alone." He waved his revolver again as if it were a victory flag. "I'll be taking you and Keenan with me."

KEENAN FINISHED HIS conversation with his FBI buddy. Dwayne Evans had been informative. While the agent hadn't any news on Isadora's whereabouts or Grant Gaines's alibi, he'd shared interesting news about the drug cartel that had infiltrated Alligator Cove. The drug cartel that Harley Broussard now owed a cool twenty-four thousand dollars.

Keenan was eager to share the news with Josette, before he told Detective Hyde that he'd likely figured out their so-called kidnapper. He walked into the kitchen, where he found Lorraine spreading peanut butter on a slice of bread.

Evidently, someone with authority had added her to the list to be admitted into the house tonight. Most likely Antoine. It was his house.

"Tired of shrimp and crab?" Keenan asked.

She didn't look up from her task. "Always get this way about the end of the day on Fat Tuesday."

"Makes sense. Have you seen Josette?"

"Last I saw of her she was heading down the hallway to the bedrooms. Harley joined her there." She shrugged, as if she was too absorbed in her sandwich to care less.

"Harley Broussard? What—"

Lorraine snarked, "I never ask too many questions at a time like that."

Keenan's heart began to pound at the thought of Josette in a back room with Harley. A desperate man in big-time trouble. He was a cocked gun. Ready to go off at any time. What could be more dangerous than stealing from a major drug cartel? Broussard was likely on more than one hit list.

Keeping his voice modulated despite the fear that threatened to overtake him, Keenan called down the hallway. A stifled female cry answered. Keenan fought the urge to charge down the hallway and start shooting, but he couldn't take the risk, not with Josette in there. He pulled his Smith and Wesson and slowly approached the closed door. "Mind if I come in?"

"No… Yes. Please."

Her voice broke. She was in trouble.

Keenan put his full weight behind him and rammed the door. The door flew open, crashing against the wall.

Harley fired, just as Keenan shot the weapon from Harley's hand.

Blood splattered the walls and Harley shouted curses. Everything moved at lightning speed as he spun around. He pulled Josette in front of him and that's when Keenan spotted a second gun. It was aimed right at Josette's head.

Her tear-filled eyes looked straight at him, pleading for help. Throughout this entire ordeal, this was the one sight Keenan wished he'd never see. Josette in danger. At that moment, he knew he'd give anything to get her to safety. Even his own life.

"Let her go, Broussard. You'll never get out of here alive. There are cops everywhere."

The gunman didn't waver. He pressed the barrel of the revolver closer to Josette's temple and she whimpered. "Maybe not but I'm taking her out with me."

Keenan knew there was no reasoning with a half-crazed, desperate gunman on a cartel's hit list. Broussard was a dead man, either way, whether it be from Keenan's weapon or the drug cartel's.

In the window he faced, he saw a shadow in the moonlight. His eyes flicked to peer more closely and he thought he recognized Hyde outside talking on the phone, alone. Could he get Hyde to turn and see the standoff without alerting Broussard? His gaze must have lingered on the window a second too long, because Broussard noticed.

His eyes diverted to the window and that was all the room Keenan needed. He fired his weapon.

Josette fell to the ground.

"ARE YOU SURE you're okay?" Keenan asked for about the tenth time since he'd carried Josette out of the blood-splattered bedroom. There was chaos all around them, cops and EMTs coming and going.

"I'm great, thanks to my valiant and brave protector," she replied. "I wasn't afraid. I knew you'd save me."

"You looked a little afraid for a minute there."

"Afraid for you," she said as they sat beside each other on the porch step. "Harley had two guns to your one."

"Well, I'm man enough to admit you scared me. When I saw that gun to your head..." He couldn't finish the thought. "Please don't ever scare me like that again."

"I'll try not to." She leaned her shoulder against his. "I wouldn't want to upset the man I love," Josette whispered.

He'd never smiled so big, never felt such happiness at hearing a few little words. Without a moment's hesitation, he kissed her, right there in the middle of mass confusion, with everyone watching.

DETECTIVE MAX HYDE was the official in charge and he orchestrated the first responders on the scene.

Harley Broussard was quickly loaded into an ambulance and taken away, sirens blazing and emergency lights flashing. He'd lost a lot of blood, but the paramedics were confident he'd pull through. Come through and face time in prison.

Josette was grateful it wasn't Keenan on that

stretcher. When the gunfire erupted, she'd been afraid to open her eyes and see him bleeding. Or worse, dead. She didn't know how she'd go on without him.

But now, as it became clear that the kidnapping was nothing but a fraud, Josette had to face another truth. Her beautiful mother was not coming home tonight. She might not ever be coming home.

Keenan wrapped his arms around her, no doubt feeling her desolation. "We'll find her, Josette. Hyde won't give up and neither will I."

She forced a smile, though tears threatened to spill down her cheeks. She needed his comfort but right now there was something else she needed more.

Antoine sat by himself, at the wooden picnic table at the edge of the bayou. His shoulders were slumped, his head hanging down. He barely looked up when she walked over and sat beside him.

"I know, Dad." It was all she said. All she had to say.

He took her hand and squeezed it and they sat in silence.

Josette knew neither of them would ever be the same without Isadora Guillory.

THE NIGHT MUSIC finally settled into a peaceful cadence that seemed to have a million tree frogs singing to the moon. It was hours later and Keenan was starting to feel as if he had overstayed his welcome. There was no kidnapping. And now the wedding he'd come for was over.

Keenan hesitated to even wonder what would have happened if the wedding had been without complications. There would have been no excuses for all the time he and Josette spent one on one. There would have still been his bum leg. That might have brought them some special time together like that first night on her balcony, but they would have missed so many other possibilities.

Now it was up to him to make sure his time with Josette would never play out.

After all, everybody needed an FBI agent on their team.

Not debating his action any longer, he walked over to where Josette sat with her father. The sad look on her face nearly broke his heart. He struggled to find the right words and opened his mouth to speak them when he noticed Detective Hyde watching them from the porch. The way he leaned so casually against the beam and the half smile on his face seemed so out of place, Keenan couldn't drag his eyes away. What was Hyde thinking?

THE NIGHT SKY looked like a velvet carpet studded with diamonds. Max walked down the porch steps and stood looking up at it. He'd never noticed how beautiful it was before.

It's perfect, he thought. The perfect setting for the surprise he had coming next, though he'd had little to do with the planning of this. It was all Isadora.

At the sound of a motor, he turned to the road-way. He watched closely, a smile breaking across his face, as the white limo pulled up and stopped near the front steps.

The uniformed driver got out, opened the rear door and stepped back as an auburn-haired woman in a silk dress stepped out.

She looked resplendent and he couldn't take his eyes off her.

The stars were no longer the brightest jewels of the night. Isadora Guillory was.

THE PARTY LASTED into the wee hours of the morning. The surprise and joy went through stages, from tears to laughter to hugs to promises and back again. Josette loved every second of every stage. Her heart had never felt this light. Her mother was safe and she was back.

Josette poured Isadora a fresh glass of bubbly as they sat at a picnic table outside, lively music playing in the background, twinkle lights illuminating the area. "I still can't believe you timed this so well, right down to the fake kidnapping."

"That, I had no control over. If I had, we could have all jumped on Harley." She looked over at Keenan. "Not that it looked like you needed any help. Let's hear it for the FBI." She held up her champagne flute.

"And the toasts just roll off her tongue," Keenan said.

"Years of Jill Hawthorne's vocabulary speaking for me," Isadora explained with a grin.

"Speaking of *The Winds of Scandal*," Antoine asked her, "did you work out your return with the producers?"

"No, I'm afraid poor Jill is the victim of no return."

Her father's face was a mixture of shock and happiness. "You're kidding. You're actually leaving *Scandal*?"

"That's the plan."

"Why?" Antoine asked her.

"I've found myself after all these years. It's right here with my family. I'm not dropping out of the business. I'm just shifting my priorities a little."

"Was that your decision?" Josette asked, shocked to hear those words from her mother's lips.

"Mine and an extremely talented new male lead for a hilarious new weekly sitcom I'm producing but not starring in."

Antoine stopped smiling. "Sounds as if I'm being replaced by a younger man this time instead of a TV show."

"Could be," Isadora said, ever the mysterious one. "If someone will hand me my handbag, I'll show you his picture."

And here they go again. Josette couldn't bear to see her dad hurt over another walk-in part that meant nothing when all was said and done. She handed her mother the handbag and then stepped away from the table. Her father started laughing. So did Keenan. It would be incredibly rude to ignore them so she went back to check out the new star. She didn't have to like him, she told herself.

A minute later she had caught the fever.

The "younger man" was a kid, maybe five or six years old. He was trying to stand on his head and failing miserably. In another picture, he was wearing a hat that was two sizes too big for him. He could barely see from under the brim. In another, he was trying to tug Isadora into a rain puddle with him.

He looked adorable. Isadora, however, looked thin and pale. She was wearing a hospital gown of sorts, fortunately one with a front and a back.

Isadora reached across the table and retrieved the photographs, then stood and turned away before the barrage of questions started.

"When was that picture taken, the one of you in the hospital gown?" Josette asked her.

"Late last March."

"That would have been just weeks after you left here," Antoine said. "Why didn't you let any of us know you'd become ill?"

"Because I didn't find out after I left. I knew before I left. I worked with a team of very highly regarded cancer specialists in Germany. They'd had excellent results." She stood up and spread out her arms in an elaborate gesture, as if she were onstage.

Cancer? Josette hated that her mother had endured that horrible disease. But before she could ask the details, her father spoke. He was obviously none too pleased.

"Fortunately you lived, but you might have died," Antoine complained. "We wouldn't have been there for you. You would have died alone."

"I invited you to go. Remember?"

"I remember well," Antoine said. "But there was never any mention of cancer."

"You had your own lives to live," she explained, looking from Antoine to Josette and back. "I'm not blaming you for anything, but I finally realized how many times I hadn't been there for you. I'd left for months at a time, frequently with no way for you to get in touch with me if you had needed something. I couldn't ask you to give up months of your lives when the medical team only gave me 30 percent odds."

Josette vacillated between concern and anger. "Why didn't you call one of us, Mom? Let us know you weren't kidnaped or killed?"

Isadora closed her eyes for a moment and when she opened them, Josette could see the anguish in their depths. "I tried to, several times. But the treatment made me so weak. And I knew there was no way I could make you believe I was all right." She huffed. "Even I'm not that good an actress."

"But, Mom, we would have been there for you. Cancer…?"

"Yes. A stomach cancer that is tough to conquer. But I beat it and I'll tell you all about it, just not now. Tonight is for all the good things I missed, including how Josette found the marvelous new addition to our family." She looked at Keenan and smiled. "You are part of the family, aren't you?"

"As long as your beautiful daughter doesn't kick me out."

"I'll vouch for him," Antoine said. "He's a keeper."

"I want to hear everything" Josette said, "especially the bit about having the adorable new star around and having a lot more of you. But right now I need some sleep."

"Plenty of room to stay here," Isadora offered.

"Thanks, but I think I have a date night, assuming we can stay awake long enough to drive home."

"There's a white limo and a driver waiting on you if you fear you can't. We have them booked until tomorrow morning at five."

"We'll take you up on that offer," Keenan said. "I thank you and so does my leg."

Josette got up, then suddenly stopped. "Before we go, there's one thing I still don't understand."

"What is it, darling?" Isadora asked.

"How did you—"

"Arrange this reunion?" her mother finished for her. "That was the easy part. I phoned Max a few hours before I got here and told him I was on my way and to make the arrangements. He said no arrangements were needed. You were all here."

Josette couldn't believe it. "You called Max Hyde? Why didn't you call Dad?"

"I wanted to surprise you and I figured it was only right to alert Max since he's been looking for me for a year."

Josette remembered Keenan telling her Max was on the phone outside the window when Harley held her at gunpoint. Was that the call? Little did her mother know, her phone call had probably saved her life. And possibly Keenan's, as well.

They said their good-nights with more hugs and

she and Keenan climbed into the limo. Josette looked back, thrilled at the sight of her parents dancing cheek to cheek in the moonlight. Even *The Winds of Scandal* couldn't produce a more perfect scene than that.

Watch it and weep, Grant Gaines.

Chapter Twenty-One

Keenan fit the magnetic key into the lock and opened the door to the Princess Suite. "I can't believe we're coming home in the wee hours two nights in a row."

Josette kicked out of her shoes. "I can't believe we're coming back to the hotel together period. Just us. No detectives. No paparazzi. No ransom. And for the first time in over a year, no worrying half the night about Isadora. That'll change tomorrow, though, when word gets out that she's here. It'll be chaos, so we'd better enjoy this quiet time."

"I know you're thrilled to have her back."

"More excited than you can imagine. What did you think?" Josette unzipped her black slacks.

"I think she's as exciting and beautiful as you said she was. Still no match for you, though." He gave her a grin. "Can you take those clothes off a little faster? It'll be daylight soon."

"It is awfully late. We can wait and make love tomorrow after some sleep if you want."

"Sure, let's do that. What's one more night to wait?"

That wasn't what Josette had expected to hear,

though she'd warned herself over and over again that something this perfect couldn't last forever.

"I'll get a quick shower," she said, trying her best to hide her disappointment. "Don't wait up for me." She closed the bedroom door, stripped and stepped into the shower.

The frosted glass door opened seconds later. A naked hunk joined her. "God, you look beautiful," he said as his hungry eyes ran over every inch of her. "I think I'd have exploded if I'd had to wait another night."

He soaped her body all over, his fingers tickling her nipples, his hands rolling across her stomach then sliding between her legs. She felt the orgasm start deep inside her and knew she'd never be able to wait for him.

She didn't have to.

"Take me," she pleaded. "Take me now."

She took his erection in her hands and guided him to her. When he entered her, she felt heat infuse her every cell. Lifting her up, he pressed her against the tiled wall and she locked her legs around him. He moved against her and she matched his rhythm, as if they'd made love for years. He captured her mouth in a heated kiss that stifled her cries as passion exploded inside her and he brought her to sweet but fierce fulfillment.

They made love twice more that night and woke to craving more a few hours later.

He wrapped his arms around her and cradled her

against his chest. She felt his heart beat beneath her cheek.

"Marry me, Josette. Today. Tomorrow. Sooner. I don't want to go home without you."

How she loved hearing those words. But there were things they needed to work out. "You live in DC. I'm in Nashville. How can we make marriage work?"

He hooked a finger under her chin and lifted her face up to his. "We'll work it out," he said as he dropped a kiss to her nose. "Distance is only a problem if we let it be."

"But you're still FBI. I'm red-carpet dresses. You're counterterrorism. I'm sequins and silk. With all those differences how can we win?"

He shifted on top of her, his arousal pressing into her. "With this much love binding us together, how can we lose?"

She had no argument for that. So she said yes and they made love again.

* * * * *

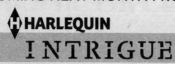

Get 4 FREE REWARDS!

We'll send you 2 FREE Books plus 2 FREE Mystery Gifts.

FREE Value Over **$20**

Both the **Harlequin Intrigue®** and **Harlequin® Romantic Suspense** series feature compelling novels filled with heart-racing action-packed romance that will keep you on the edge of your seat.

YES! Please send me 2 FREE novels from the Harlequin Intrigue or Harlequin Romantic Suspense series and my 2 FREE gifts (gifts are worth about $10 retail). After receiving them, if I don't wish to receive any more books, I can return the shipping statement marked "cancel." If I don't cancel, I will receive 6 brand-new Harlequin Intrigue Larger-Print books every month and be billed just $6.49 each in the U.S. or $6.99 each in Canada, a savings of at least 13% off the cover price, or 4 brand-new Harlequin Romantic Suspense books every month and be billed just $5.49 each in the U.S. or $6.24 each in Canada, a savings of at least 12% off the cover price. It's quite a bargain! Shipping and handling is just 50¢ per book in the U.S. and $1.25 per book in Canada.* I understand that accepting the 2 free books and gifts places me under no obligation to buy anything. I can always return a shipment and cancel at any time by calling the number below. The free books and gifts are mine to keep no matter what I decide.

Choose one: ☐ **Harlequin Intrigue**   ☐ **Harlequin Romantic Suspense**
              Larger-Print   (240/340 HDN GRJK)
              (199/399 HDN GRJK)

Name (please print)

Address   Apt. #

City   State/Province   Zip/Postal Code

Email: Please check this box ☐ if you would like to receive newsletters and promotional emails from Harlequin Enterprises ULC and its affiliates. You can unsubscribe anytime.

Mail to the Harlequin Reader Service:
IN U.S.A.: P.O. Box 1341, Buffalo, NY 14240-8531
IN CANADA: P.O. Box 603, Fort Erie, Ontario L2A 5X3

Want to try 2 free books from another series! Call 1-800-873-8635 or visit www.ReaderService.com.

*Terms and prices subject to change without notice. Prices do not include sales taxes, which will be charged (if applicable) based on your state or country of residence. Canadian residents will be charged applicable taxes. Offer not valid in Quebec. This offer is limited to one order per household. Books received may not be as shown. Not valid for current subscribers to the Harlequin Intrigue or Harlequin Romantic Suspense series. All orders subject to approval. Credit or debit balances in a customer's account(s) may be offset by any other outstanding balance owed by or to the customer. Please allow 4 to 6 weeks for delivery. Offer available while quantities last.

Your Privacy—Your information is being collected by Harlequin Enterprises ULC, operating as Harlequin Reader Service. For a complete summary of the information we collect, how we use this information and to whom it is disclosed, please visit our privacy notice located at corporate.harlequin.com/privacy-notice. From time to time we may also exchange your personal information with reputable third parties. If you wish to opt out of this sharing of your personal information, please visit readerservice.com/consumerschoice or call 1-800-873-8635. **Notice to California Residents**—Under California law, you have specific rights to control and access your data. For more information on these rights and how to exercise them, visit corporate.harlequin.com/california-privacy.

HIHRS22R3

HARLEQUIN
PLUS

Try the best multimedia subscription service for romance readers like you!

Read, Watch and Play.

Experience the easiest way to get the romance content you crave.

Start your **FREE TRIAL** at
<u>www.harlequinplus.com/freetrial</u>.